Truth *and* lies

Jonathon stood in the middle of the room. "So, Mina, president of the honor society now?"

I stared over his shoulder at the door.

Jonathon stepped closer. "And still going to Harvard?" He laughed.

I could feel the back of my throat beginning to close.

Jonathon took another step. He leaned forward, his chest pressing against my waist. "Come on, Mina," he whispered. "I was only joking. You know that. Right? I've missed you. How come you haven't been returning my calls?" Jonathon circled his arms around me.

I pried his hands from my waist and walked quickly to the door.

Jonathon followed me. "Hey, Mina. Stop." He reached out and held the door closed. "Just wait a minute, will you?"

I closed my eyes. "I have to go, Jonathon."

Jonathon pulled back his hand. "Fine. You can leave if you want to. I just wanted to talk about what you're going to tell your mother when she finds out you've been lying."

OTHER SPEAK BOOKS

wait *for* me

AN NA

speak

An Imprint of Penguin Group (USA) Inc.

11

F

SPEAK
Published by the Penguin Group
Penguin Group (USA) Inc., 345 Hudson Street, New York, New York 10014, U.S.A.
Penguin Group (Canada), 90 Eglinton Avenue East, Suite 700, Toronto, Ontario, Canada M4P 2Y3
(a division of Pearson Penguin Canada Inc.)
Penguin Books Ltd, 80 Strand, London WC2R 0RL, England
Penguin Ireland, 25 St Stephen's Green, Dublin 2, Ireland (a division of Penguin Books Ltd)
Penguin Group (Australia), 250 Camberwell Road, Camberwell, Victoria 3124, Australia
(a division of Pearson Australia Group Pty Ltd)
Penguin Books India Pvt Ltd, 11 Community Centre, Panchsheel Park, New Delhi - 110 017, India
Penguin Group (NZ), 67 Apollo Drive, Rosedale, North Shore 0745, Auckland, New Zealand
(a division of Pearson New Zealand Ltd.)
Penguin Books (South Africa) (Pty) Ltd, 24 Sturdee Avenue,
Rosebank, Johannesburg 2196, South Africa

First published in the United States of America by G. P. Putnam's Sons,
a division of Penguin Young Readers Group, 2006
Published by Speak, an imprint of Penguin Group (USA) Inc., 2007

10 9 8 7 6 5 4 3 2 1

Copyright © An Na, 2006

THE LIBRARY OF CONGRESS HAS CATALOGED THE G. P. PUTNAM'S SONS EDITION AS FOLLOWS:
Na, An, 1972–   Wait for me / An Na.   p. cm.
ISBN: 0-399-24275-9 (hc)
Summary: As her senior year in high school approaches, Mina yearns to find her own path in life
but working at the family business, taking care of her little sister, and dealing with her mother's
impossible expectations are as stifling as the southern California heat,
until she falls in love with a man who offers a way out.
[1. Self-actualization (Psychology)—Fiction. 2. Mothers and daughters—Fiction.
3. Sisters—Fiction. 4. Korean Americans—Fiction. 5. Hearing impaired—Fiction.
6. California—Fiction.] I. Title.   PZ7.N1243Wai 2006   [Fic]—dc22   2005030931

Speak ISBN 978-0-14-240918-3

Printed in the United States of America

For my brother
Sung An
1976–2003

wait *for* me

prologue

She walks alone in the rain. The faded pink pajama bottoms and oversized T-shirt clinging to her small frame, heavy with the weight of water. Her breath breaks inside her chest in an upward heave that strangles a cry escaping from her throat. Gulps of air. Her shoulders rising and falling. How much time has passed? She presses the heel of her hand against the tears that blur her vision. Though her chest still throbs, demanding air, she begins to run again. Looks down at her feet and urges them to fly faster, skim across the pavement.

The city, a dusty camouflage of grays punctuated with dots of colors from traffic lights and swirling neon signs, stretches awake in the early-morning drizzle. In the distance there is the slam of metal gates being pushed aside, revealing cluttered storefronts and display windows. The heartbeat of the city thickens with the heat of summer rising as steam from the streets, with the noise of cars speeding across the freeway, with the multitude of voices and languages rising up to greet each other. The day begins, yet all Suna can see is the memory of a face framed by night. A face so familiar, so loved, she can name each imperfection, each mark as though they are her own.

Suna runs forward without a glance, without a thought. To the car rounding the curve of the freeway off-ramp. The road slick with oil and rain. She pumps her arms and wills herself into the light.

mina

I found her sleeping on the couch, her body curled to one side, her head lodged against the faded green armrest. I pushed her damp bangs off her forehead and whispered in her good ear. "Suna."

She stirred in her sleep, an arm flung up over her head. Her stuffed dog peeked out from under her neck.

"Suna." I dangled her hearing aid in front of her, letting it bump against her forehead. Her eyes remained closed. I gently shook her shoulder. "Suna, wake up."

Her eyes fluttered and then finally opened. She looked blankly into my face for a moment before a smile skimmed across her lips.

"Hi, Uhn-nee," she said and rubbed the sleep from her eyes using the back of her hand, fingers curled like a baby. If only she knew how young she looked when she did that, she would have stopped instantly. She was always protesting that she wasn't a baby anymore, this sister of mine. Certainly a baby couldn't start middle school. She had been certain that the summer would work magic. Make her grow in all the right places. And here it was the beginning of August and my old training bra was still in the dresser.

Suna sat up and moved to one side so that I could sit down. I kicked out my legs to rest them on the coffee table and dropped the hearing aid into her lap. In a practiced gesture, Suna held her hair back with one hand and dropped her chin as she hooked the larger molded plastic amplifier behind her ear and inserted the smaller piece into the canal. She smoothed her hair back over her ear.

"I'm going to chain you to your bed if you don't stop sleepwalking," I joked even as I thought seriously about taking her to the doctor at the clinic. The sleepwalking had been kind of funny at first, but when it didn't stop, it started to freak me out. Sometimes if I caught her as she was getting out of bed, she seemed completely awake. Eyes open and everything.

"Did Uhmma and Apa leave already?" Suna asked. She glanced behind her to the kitchen as though expecting them to be eating.

"A long time ago," I said and checked my watch. Seven A.M. "Come on." I stood up. "It's late. Uhmma's gonna be pissed if we don't hurry up."

A dry cleaning business set time by the rising sun. And there were never enough hands. With the business so slow the last few years, there wasn't money to hire employees. Uhmma and Apa relied on us, and mostly me, to help out at every opportunity. Before school, after school, during vacations and summers.

As Suna and I walked toward the car, I could almost see the tiny waves of heat trapped inside, ready to bake us alive. As soon as we opened the doors, the hot air poured out, pooling around our legs. Suna and I furiously rolled down the windows and adjusted the beach towels that kept the backs of our thighs from being scorched by the hot vinyl. I tossed my ponytail over one shoulder and jammed the key into the ignition.

"Wait, Uhn-nee!" Suna shouted.

I sighed and slouched in my seat. Suna closed her eyes and began to mutter, talking to the car she had named Sally. The white Nissan Sentra was older than God, but Suna believed it just needed some coaxing.

"Okay," Suna said after a minute.

"Sally said she'd work for us today?" I asked and smiled.

"I told her I'd wash her windows if she was good." Suna quickly patted the burning-hot dashboard, then blew on her hand. She treated the car like a pet, rewarding it when everything ran smoothly, gently chiding when we had to take it in for service. It all started the day she learned that plants responded to music and talking. No matter how much I tried to reason with her, she continued talking to the car.

I turned the ignition and held my breath. These last few days had been so odd. What with the Santa Ana winds starting up so early in the middle of summer instead of the fall, Suna sleepwalking, the washing machines breaking down. Everything felt off balance.

Sally sputtered to life, her guttural engine barely catching. One more day. Already the sweat pooled behind my knees and trickled down my calves. I turned on the radio and eased out of the parking space, slowly driving over the three speed bumps that led out of the apartment complex, then turned on to the main street.

El Cajon Boulevard. Six lanes of black asphalt stretching far into the horizon, shimmering with waves of heat. Strip malls lined up on either side with their garish painted signs. A song about summer came on. Something about soaking up the sun. What a joke. But I started to sing along. Loud as I could until Suna broke into laughter. It always amazed me how music could take me to another place. It didn't matter if I was at church singing in the chorus about God or jamming to the radio or listening to my CDs. Even the most insipid song had something. A beat, a melody, that lone bass holding everything together. But when a song was right, when everything fell together, each note, each rise and dip of the voice filled me with a sense of yearning. A vastness. The sensation of flight seeping into my skin until I was skimming through the air, the music holding me aloft.

Red light. Even this early on a summer day, the migrant workers stood on the corners, waiting for work. For a pickup truck to slow down and stop, a pale arm reaching out the window, motioning for two or three to hop in back. I didn't understand how they could stand to be dressed in those plaid button-down long-sleeve shirts and jeans. Weren't they dying in all those clothes? The light turned green and I sped past.

I flipped on the right turn signal, eased the car into the

parking lot of one of the strip malls. I could see Uhmma through the glass walls of the dry cleaners. She was at the front, looking through the cash register.

"Damn." I stepped on the brake. "What is she doing?"

I turned the wheel too quickly, making Sally squeal in protest, and parked in the alley behind Uhmma and Apa's van.

Suna turned in her seat to look at me.

I sat still for a moment and stared at the open back door of the dry cleaners. What were the chances? What was the worst Uhmma could do? There was plenty, but would she even know from looking at the receipts? I had been the only one to handle them since the beginning of summer. I cursed under my breath. I should have doctored them yesterday. It was too late now.

"Come on," I said, and Suna and I stepped out of the car and walked toward the dry cleaners. Even in this heat, walking into the store was like stepping from the clouds straight into hell.

suna

Suna sticks her arm out the window, pushing her hand through the hot air as the car speeds down the street. Her hand dives down, then up, down, up, a roller-coaster ride, a kite on the beach. The wind whips back her shoulder-length hair, making her smile at the way it flies around her head as though disconnected from her body. Suna hears her sister singing and though Mina is but an arm's reach away, Mina's voice must travel oceans before Suna can register the voice she knows like it is her own. It has always been like this. Since she was a baby. And even with the hearing aid, the sounds of the world filter into her mind tinny and light as a wind chime swinging in a breeze.

Suna closes her eyes, tries to guess which store they are going to pass next. Tan to Tan, she whispers to herself and opens her eyes. Two stores too early. They are only at Oriental Nails II. She closes her eyes to try again. Red light. Open.

He sits at the bus bench. Not on the seat, but on top of

the backrest, his feet splayed out on the bench, elbows on his knees, shoulders hunched forward, hands clasped in front. She can't quite see his eyes, his cap is pulled down too low. But she notices a scar the size of half an orange etched just to the right of his chin. Like a crescent moon, Suna thinks.

Moon says something out of the corner of his lips. The man next to him shakes his head no, then says something to make Moon smile, his scar flattening, stretching until it almost seems like a dimple. Maybe it is the sound of their radio or the way Suna's arm is draped out the window, but Moon lifts his eyes. To the street. To the car. For her. Suna freezes, unable to look away. Caught in his gaze. In the lightning-flash smile breaking across his face. He nods hello. Green light.

Suna closes her eyes and tries to recapture the moment. She holds his face like a point of light suspended against the darkness.

From across the oceans, Suna hears her older sister's voice, senses Mina sitting up straighter. And then he is gone. Lost to the day. Suna returns for Mina.

mina

I braced myself for Uhmma's anger, walking quickly through the back of the store, dodging all the plastic-wrapped clothes suspended from the conveyor belt, and headed straight for the problem.

"Hi, Uhmma," I said as casually as possible.

My mother looked up from the receipts and frowned at my shorts and tank top. A lecture about the kind of clothes I was supposed to wear when I was working up front parted Uhmma's lips, but then she changed her mind and instead waved some receipts.

Mina, have you checked these numbers? Uhmma asked in Korean while looking over the slips.

I placed my backpack on top of the counter and answered back in Korean, hoping to keep on Uhmma's good side.

Here, Uhmma, I said and took the receipts from her. I have not had a chance to go over them. They are still unorganized. I will put them in order after I study for my SATs.

The subject of my SATs immediately turned Uhmma's attention away from the receipts. Have you been practicing? she asked.

I nodded and took out my practice books to show her. Uhmma glanced at the red covers and nodded.

Remember, Mina, Uhmma started lecturing, you do not have another chance. Your senior year is very important. Mrs. Kim says that Jonathon only got into Stanford after he got a perfect score on his SAT. Which reminds me, Mrs. Kim has more books for you. From that expensive preparation class Jonathon took last summer.

I quietly nodded, but grabbed the counter, forcing all my hatred into the wood instead of my face. Mrs. Kim could go to hell and take along her pimply son, Jonathon. I had grown to hate him as much as Uhmma idolized him.

Jonathon and I had known each other since we were little kids and our families had met at church. Uhmma looked up to Mrs. Kim and called her older sister. It seemed like all my life everything the Kims did was perfect. Their beautiful house, their successful restaurant, the respect people showed them at church. Even after Mr. Kim passed away from a heart attack, the way Mrs. Kim continued to run their Korean restaurant and the way Jonathon had stepped up like a responsible man, taking over the books and managing the employees, was all an example for me. This was how a good, respectable family lived.

Jonathon, unlike me, had time to himself. He managed the restaurant's finances and helped on busy weekend nights, but he never had the daily grind because he could afford to hire people. I barely had enough time to make a few after-school meetings for chorus and clubs, and that was only because Uhmma knew it looked good on college applications. I had long ago stopped asking to go out with school friends and they had stopped asking me to come along. Which was fine with Uhmma, since she thought my church friends were better. But even that had been taken from me. I could picture Jonathon with my old crowd of friends at church. The way he watched me as I walked across the parking lot, trying to avoid him. From the way the group whispered and cut their eyes at me, I knew he had told them things. About me. About us.

I put away my books, placed the receipts in a manila envelope and shoved it under the counter. I turned to Uhmma and asked with dread, Do I have to pick up the books from Mrs. Kim?

She frowned. I do not believe she has any time today. She is so busy helping Jonathon get ready for Stanford.

Uhmma wheeled a bin of dirty clothes toward the back of the store. Mina, she called out, bring me those shirts by the sewing machine.

Yes, Uhmma, I answered and leaned back against the counter in relief. I had been getting careless. I needed to make sure that all my numbers were in order before I left the register each day. I could just imagine how understanding Uhmma would be if I told her I had decided to pay myself for all the work I did. That I was saving it for something important. I picked up the shirts and took them to the back.

Suna stood to one side of the machines, waiting to help load. Uhmma began sorting the clothes, looking over every inch of the garments for stains. She dropped clothes into piles depending on which stain remover she would have to apply before the washing. Suna pulled a dress from the bin and dropped it into a pile beside Uhmma. She reached in for another item. Uhmma bent down and picked up the dress that Suna had just placed there and shook her head. She shoved Suna's hands out of the way.

Go, Uhmma ordered. Go help Apa.

Suna nodded, her lower lip caught between her teeth.

Apa sat on his stool, methodically placing an ironed shirt on a stand with a hook, pulling the plastic wrap over the shirt and then holding on to the hanger as he pressed a foot pedal that lowered the stand with a loud bang. He handed the hanger to Suna, who hung it on a conveyor belt suspended from the ceiling. Apa lifted the stand back up and hung another shirt on the hook. With each bang, with each bend of his back, Apa exhaled loudly.

Suna placed a hand on Apa's shoulder, speaking softly in Korean. Apa, let me do this.

Yah, Suna, I am not an old man yet, Apa said.

Let me sit down. My legs are tired, Suna lied.

Apa glanced at her face, worry creasing his forehead. Did you get enough sleep? You were on the couch again this morning, Suna-ya. I do not like you wandering around at night like that.

I cannot help it, Apa. It just happens in my sleep. Suna gingerly took his elbow, trying to help him up to his feet.

Just this time, Apa said and slowly unfurled his long frame, knees creaking, back straightening. He stood and smiled down at Suna, patting her back.

Uhmma shook a shirt in my face. Mina! Mina!

"What?" I said with a scowl, turning back to Uhmma.

You are not paying attention. Uhmma waved a woman's silk blouse in my face before throwing it into the pile with oil stains.

If I wanted a poor job done, I would have had your sister help, she said.

I bit the inside of my cheek to keep from yelling back at Uhmma's comment. I caught Suna's eye and made an evil face at Uhmma's back. Suna tried to smile, but her eyes were rimmed with tears.

Sometimes when I looked at Suna, I could feel my heart break. Suna had always been a sickly baby. Always catching one cold after another. Uhmma couldn't stand Suna's constant crying and need for attention. When it became too much, Uhmma walked to her bedroom, head bowed, her hands over her ears.

Once, I came home from school to find Suna's small one-year-old body so tired from crying, she could barely crawl over to me. So I carried Suna as only a seven-year-old can, under her arms, her back pressed to my chest, her feet dragging along the kitchen floor. I found a bowl, poured some milk and offered it to my sister as though she were a cat. And only when she was unable to lap it up did I raise the bowl to her lips, tipping it forward, sloshing the milk against her chin. I joyfully watched her drink.

So really, what was the use in getting angry? What did I expect from Uhmma? I went back to sorting the clothes.

suna

Suna feels her father patting her back and turns to watch him walk slowly over to one of the broken washing machines. She turns back to covering the shirts. Mina and Uhmma continue sorting the soiled clothes, their silence punctuated with angry snips. They are always fighting. Suna quickly finishes the shirts and escapes into the forest of clothes. As she walks away, she reaches up and carefully removes her hearing aid. The hard plastic device shoved deep into her pocket.

The shrouded pressed garments hang from a conveyor belt, their ghostly forms reminding her of the floating jellyfish she once saw at an aquarium. Suna weaves in and out of the clothes, pretending for a moment that she is underwater. A fan rustles the gossamer sheeting, sending ripples through her ocean.

From her murky hiding place, she watches her mother waving some clothes at her sister, one slender hand on her hip. Mina unknowingly does the same. Their profiles mirror each other, same high cheekbones, angular noses, but Mina has different lips. Where her mother's are rather thin and sharp, her sister's are full, generous. Mina has a habit of chewing her bottom lip, and for many years, when Suna was younger, she had believed that this was the secret to her sister's lips. So Suna copied Mina's habit until her mother sharply reprimanded her. And then she had to resort to biting them at night before she fell asleep. Even after she realized that her lips would never resemble her sister's, she still found herself biting the thin flesh of her lower lip when she had trouble falling asleep.

Suna turns her back on them. She can tell by the curve of Uhmma's lips that she is talking about her again. Talking about all the ways that Suna does not measure up. Suna tries to remember a time when Uhmma was not angry with her. A time when Uhmma did not grimace when Suna had to adjust her hearing aid or ask someone to repeat themselves. Suna tries to remember, but keeps coming back to Mina. Mina holding her hand as they walked across the uneven grass of the church's lawn. Mina yanking the back of her dress as she started to cross the street while a car was coming. Mina brushing the hair off her forehead to wake her up.

If only she could disappear. Part the clothes and step into another world. Like Narnia. She holds her breath and brings her hands together, palm to palm. Pushes them out in front as though diving through the water. She slips through.

mina

*I*t'll be ready for you on Wednesday," I said and circled the day and the total before carefully tearing the bottom portion of the receipt off along its perforation. I handed the tag to the woman and pinned a corresponding number to her dress.

"Thanks," she said, shoving the tag into her wallet.

I watched the woman walk out of the store. Her blue suit could have used some tailoring, the waist taken in slightly, the sleeves shortened, but most people didn't know any better. They figured that if they didn't bulge out in all the wrong places, then the outfit must fit. I went back to totaling the receipts from yesterday. I checked behind me to make sure no one was around and then quickly reached into the register and took three twenties. Depending on the day and how much business we had, I took more or less. Jonathon, who showed me how to alter the receipts when we first started studying together, also taught me not to be too greedy. That was how you got caught.

After returning the receipts to the manila folder, I headed back to the office to see if Suna wanted to go for some lunch. A loud groan from behind one of the machines turned my steps.

Apa? I called out, leaning to one side, trying to peer behind the forest of clothes. Apa? I called again, unable to see him. What is the matter?

Go. Go get your uhmma. Apa's soft voice came from behind one of the machines.

I ran.

It took both Uhmma and me bearing all his weight to help him walk to the office. He immediately lay on the floor. Uhmma squatted near his shoulder and looked down at him. Her eyes traveled the length of his body as Apa squinted against the pain.

Uhmma narrowed her eyes and asked, Who told you to go crawling around behind those machines? You knew your back could not handle that kind of twisting. Is this what you wanted, to leave all the work for me? Look at you! Uhmma clucked her tongue and turned her head away as though unable to bear the sight of his old supine body.

You are like an old grandfather. An old, old grandfather. Useless, she complained.

Apa's face, which had been in such agony just moments before, suddenly, with the battering of Uhmma's words, smoothed in appearance.

Suna appeared from out of the blue, her hand reaching

up to her ear, placing in the hearing aid. She whispered to me, "Uhn-nee. Is Apa going to be okay?"

Apa opened his eyes. Turned his head slightly so that he could look over at us. He smiled in reassurance.

Uhmma shoved his shoulder, making him jerk and inhale quickly between clinched teeth.

She stood up and stepped over his body. On her way out of the office she said, He is going to live just to make me miserable.

She wouldn't speak to him for the rest of the day. Suna took him cool drinks, kneeling beside him, holding a straw up to his lips as he took long sips. I heard Uhmma calling Mrs. Kim, her voice high and soft in a singsong of flattery.

Aii, Mrs. Kim, I hate to trouble you at such a busy time, but you always have the best advice. That husband of mine, he has no sense. He hurt his back again. . . . Yes, it is very bad. He cannot even walk. . . . Yes, we will come over. Are you sure you have time? . . . If you insist, she said.

I dug my nails into my palm, trying to hold back the sickness that overwhelmed my body. I avoided Uhmma in the hopes that somehow, she would not take me with her. I stayed up front, pretending to be memorizing more vocabulary words in between customers, but each time I opened the prep books, I thought I could see traces of his fingerprints all over the pages. His fingers were always stained with blue ink. With each blue smudge, I exhaled loudly to keep from feeling the nausea, to hold back the images that surfaced with every blink. Jonathon groping at my shirt. The oily sheen on his skin as he bent down to kiss me. I had not spoken to him or returned his calls in two weeks. Not since the time I had left his house after a "study session" and I had washed my skin until it was raw. And still the sharp musk stench of his body would not come off my skin. I just couldn't do it anymore. I couldn't go on pretending, no matter what was at stake.

I spent the rest of the day at the register, staring out the floor-to-ceiling windows. I watched the lunch crowds swarm into the parking lot and then recede by late afternoon. The hot Santa Ana winds picked up the litter in the parking lot and swirled it around, lifting it up in a dance. The walls of the dry cleaners radiated heat. Sweat trickled down the back of my neck, under my arms, between my fingers.

Some of the customers spoke of a fire in the mountains. Started by arsonists, they said. "It's this heat. It gets inside your head, makes you do crazy things," a woman said to her husband.

"Not the heat," he muttered. "It's the wind."

The Santa Ana winds, hot and dry as an open oven, blazed down with the force of the sun from the high desert mountains. Blowing in fierce gusts, offering no relief, coating our bodies with dust and ill wishes. The wind blew in between cracks and stirred up the history of all that was meant to stay hidden.

suna

Suna watches her father sleeping, the angles of his face softened by dreams. Though his skin is wrinkled, it still bears the marks of his youth. She can remember as a child being fascinated by his scars. Tracing the large craters on his cheeks with her small fingers. Pressing her thumb into the deep impressions along his chin and jawline. She remembers the way her father sat so patiently as she examined him, sitting cross-legged on the carpet with the Korean newspaper spread out in front of him.

The acne scars are now withering into lines of old age. Her father has never been a young man, but lately the years seem not to creep, but stampede across his face and his body. She has never questioned the way he looks, but as she grows older, she begins to notice the way other people look at him or rather avoid looking at him. Some begin a conversation staring into his eyes but end up curiously roaming the planes of his face. Others prefer to gaze over his shoulder or keep their eyes on an object. It is only in those moments that she turns away from her father. So that she will not have to bear witness to how others perceive him. For no matter how much she loves him, she cannot help but feel the prickling heat of shame every time someone stares or pointedly looks away. Ashamed to be his daughter, ashamed for feeling that way, but mostly, ashamed for acting like her mother.

Suna had always believed it had been because her mother was so busy, but now she recognizes the way her mother walks ten steps ahead of him, even at church, avoiding any association until it is time to leave. How her mother flinches when he touches her. The easy manner her mother employs when redirecting conversations away from him. Suna fiddles with her hearing aid. She recognizes all those signs.

mina

*M*ina, Uhmma called out. Mina, get ready to go, she said.

Where are we going? I asked, playing dumb. What about Apa and Suna?

Uhmma reached up and pulled off the handkerchief that held back her dyed black hair.

We will take them home and then we must go and talk to Mrs. Kim, Uhmma said.

I stayed rooted to my stool. Why? I asked. Did you not say that Mrs. Kim was very busy with Jonathon's preparations for college?

Uhmma snapped, Do you think I want to bother Mrs. Kim? She is being generous enough to help us. If that man had not caused all this trouble . . .

Uhmma paused in her tirade to take in my outfit. She squinted slightly before reaching up to the buttons that controlled the conveyor belt. The plastic-shrouded clothes shook and moved along the belt until Uhmma released the button.

She flipped through a few of the dresses, picked one out, checked the tag and held it up against me.

No, Uhmma, I protested, shoving the dress away.

Uhmma shoved the dress back toward me. Stop it, Mina. Put it on. You look like a prostitute in those shorts and tank top.

I took a deep breath and turned away from her.

Mina-ya, Uhmma said, her tone softer, do not make me look bad in front of Mrs. Kim. I am tired. Do you not think I have enough headaches? Uhmma hung the dress on the hook near the cash register and walked to the back of the store.

The mauve stucco houses with their terra-cotta roofs and wide-leafed plantings by the front door lined the gently curved streets of Jonathon's neighborhood. I could never tell the houses apart. Each development bled into the next until all you could see from the freeway as you approached Rancho Bernardo were the rooftops, like a sea of broken clay pots stretching far into the desert landscape.

Uhmma rang the doorbell and then lightly ran her fingers along the hairline of her forehead where beads of sweat had dared to appear. She touched her fingers to the hem of her skirt. I slouched in my too starched, too lacy, too floral dress and licked the sweat off my upper lip. Uhmma narrowed her eyes at me.

The door opened.

Uhmma said brightly, "Jonathon. You get new haircut. Look so handsome. Like college man now."

Ahn-young-ha-say-yo, Mrs. Kang, Jonathon said. Please come in. He stepped back and out of the way, opening the front door.

We stepped into the marble-floored foyer and I immediately shivered from the blast of air-conditioning. Mrs. Kim called from the kitchen, Do-ru-wah-yo, Mrs. Kang.

We all walked into the large, sunny kitchen where Mrs. Kim was just placing some fruit and rice crackers on plates.

Uhmma rushed to her side and took the plates from her.

Mrs. Kim, Uhmma loudly admonished, you did not have to go to the trouble.

Mrs. Kim smiled. What trouble? Let us take the plates to the living room. She turned to Jonathon. Did you ask Mrs. Kang and Mina if they would like a drink?

Uhmma interrupted, No, no, we are not thirsty. We just came for a quick visit. We do not want to interrupt your dinner preparations.

Mrs. Kim patted the air with one hand and walked toward the living room. She said, We are never too busy for our friends. Come now, sit down.

We all followed Mrs. Kim from the kitchen to the living room. The pristine white couches faced each other, separated by a large, ornately carved coffee table. Each sofa cushion and armrest was covered with round crocheted doilies. Uhmma carefully set the fruit and rice crackers on the coffee table. Mrs. Kim sat on one of the doilies; Uhmma sat next to her on the other one. Jonathon and I took our spots on the couch across from them.

Mrs. Kim focused her eyes on me.

Mina, Mrs. Kim said, you are looking more and more like a refined young lady.

Uhmma bowed her head slightly and smiled in a demure fashion, as though she were the recipient of that dreadful compliment.

"Thanks," I said.

Uhmma shot me a quick scowl.

I sighed under my breath. To avoid the lecture, I added, Gam-sa-hahm-nee-da.

Uhmma nodded at me and added, Mina has been looking forward to her senior year. Now that she is president of the honor society, she'll be very busy this year.

Mrs. Kim's lips turned up in a slight smile that resembled more of a smirk. Oh, she is the president of the honor society now? When did that happen?

I gripped the edge of the armrest.

Uhmma frowned. Yes, remember, Mrs. Kim? I told you last week on the phone.

Oh, yes, that is right. Mrs. Kim raised her fingers to her cheek as though embarrassed to have forgotten.

Uhmma continued to brag, It is a wonder she keeps up all her straight A's while doing all that extra work at school and still finding time to help her parents. Sometimes I have to tell her to stop studying so hard and go to sleep.

Mrs. Kim leaned toward me but directed her words at Uhmma. She sighed, Mina, how I would have liked a daughter like you. A daughter who stays home. Someone to talk to. This son of mine is too busy to stay by his mother's side. He is always going out. I still do not understand how he could have gotten such good grades when he was always fooling around and going to the beach. He is too smart for his own good.

Mrs. Kim turned to Jonathon. Did you set aside the books for Mina?

Jonathon nodded.

Mrs. Kim said, The books from the preparation class raised Jonathon's score more than one hundred points.

Jonathon shifted in his seat, his eyes blinking quickly, as though his contacts were about to fall out.

Mrs. Kim kept her face toward Uhmma but said to Jonathon, Well, go get them for Mina.

Uhmma added quickly, Mina can help. Thank you so much for saving them for her.

Mrs. Kim patted the air again. Nonsense. Why should we not all help each other?

Jonathon stood up and walked back to the foyer. Uhmma took a breath to speak, but then focused her attention on me. She waited until I slowly stood up and followed after Jonathon.

Uhmma's voice in the distance commented, Jonathon is looking so handsome. Such a young man now.

Mrs. Kim complained, clucking her tongue, Ai, that boy, Mrs. Kang, sometimes he has no sense. Just the other day, at a restaurant, he goes and spills lobster soup on his best suit. On his best suit. Right before he must pack it for college. No common sense, that boy. The smell coming from that suit.

Jonathon and I climbed the stairs for his room. He stepped quickly. I willed my feet to follow. Jonathon got to the top of the stairs and went down the hall, out of sight.

He was leaning up against his desk, flipping through the SAT book when I got to his room. I stood at the open doorway.

"Come in and close the door," Jonathon said quietly.

I shifted my weight from foot to foot. "Can I just have the books? I really have to get going."

"Where do you have to go?" Jonathon asked, an incredulous look on his face.

I tried to pretend he had no clue about my life, as though he didn't know all my friends, or lack thereof, or that all I ever did was help at the dry cleaners and listen to my music. "I have this appointment," I said, trailing off.

"Yeah, right," Jonathon snorted.

"Knock it off, Jonathon. Just give me the books."

"Get them yourself," he said and threw the book in his hand across the room. It landed on the bed next to some thick binders with the same red cover.

I wanted to tell him to screw himself, he could keep his books, but those books were my passport out of his house. I knew Uhmma would not let me leave without them. I walked quickly to his bed. Jonathon stepped away from his desk and closed the door. I clenched my jaw and gathered the book and binders to my chest.

Jonathon stood in the middle of the room. "So, Mina, president of the honor society now?"

I stared over his shoulder at the door.

Jonathon stepped closer. "And still going to Harvard?" He laughed.

I could feel the back of my throat beginning to close.

Jonathon took another step. He leaned forward, his chest pressing against my wrist. "Come on, Mina," he whispered. "I was only joking. You know that. Right? I've missed you. How come you haven't been returning my calls?" Jonathon circled his arms around me.

I pried his hands from my waist and walked quickly to the door.

Jonathon followed me. "Hey, Mina. Stop." He reached out and held the door closed. "Just wait a minute, will you."

I closed my eyes. "I have to go, Jonathon."

Jonathon pulled back his hand. "Fine. You can leave if you want to. I just wanted to talk about what you're going to tell your mother when she finds out you've been lying," he said.

I held my breath, my hand quivering to reach for the doorknob.

Jonathon continued, "Because my mom knows that my friend Parker Lee is the next president of the honor society. And an ex-president would know these things, right? So how are you going to explain that to your mom after my mom tells her the truth?"

He had me. I wanted to punch the door, but instead, I turned around. My jaw was clenched so tight, my teeth hurt. I hated myself for doing it, but I finally forced myself to ask.

"What do you think?"

Jonathon sat down on the bed, his smile as wide as the headboard. "Well, we could tell her that Parker needed some help and that he asked you to co-head the honor society."

I nodded stiffly.

"What about your mom?" I asked.

Jonathon waved away my concern. "Don't worry, I already told my mom that you were co-head after your mom called my mom last week to brag."

Relief at avoiding the close call made me grateful and guilty for being such a jerk earlier. "Thanks," I whispered.

Jonathon pointed at me. "You know, Mina, you should really be more careful about what you make up. I mean, pretending that I was tutoring you while I figured out a way to forge your report card was one thing, but to say that you're president of the honor society . . . you should tell me these things beforehand so we can coordinate our stories."

I clutched the prep books closer and nodded again.

Jonathon continued, "And you have to get your mom to stop saying you're going to Harvard. It's making my mom all jealous and suspicious. She asked me, if your grades were so high, why you didn't get any awards at that awards night celebration last June."

The blood pounded against the sides of my face. If anyone could threaten the elaborate scaffolding of all my lies, it was Jonathon. The last person I wanted to trust.

"What did you say?" I asked.

Jonathon shrugged. "I just told her that the awards thing was mostly for seniors. That you would be getting plenty the next year."

I exhaled slowly. How long could I keep this up? How much longer before all my lies about my grades, about going to Harvard, crumbled around me?

Jonathon stood up and moved next to me, lightly touching my hair. "So how come you're not talking to me? Why are you acting like we didn't have something together?" Jonathon asked. "I thought things were good."

I tried not to flinch at his touch. Did he really believe that? Just thinking about what had happened that last night we were together made me want to peel the skin off my body.

I whispered, "Jonathon, you're going to college. Please. Just let it go."

The sweaty palm of his hand came to rest on the back of my neck. He spoke into my hair. "Is that why you've been avoiding me? I thought maybe you had gotten tired of using me."

I froze.

"That is what you were doing, right?" Jonathon lowered his voice even further.

I dug my fingernails into the skin of my upper arms, crushed the prep books into my chest until the edge of the binder cut into my skin. I welcomed every bit of the pain. Anything to keep from feeling the disgust at myself.

Jonathon grabbed my elbow and forced it up.

I gasped.

"What is this?" he asked, pointing to the deep red marks. "Do I disgust you that much? You have to force yourself to let me touch you?"

I wrenched my arm out of his grasp and stepped away from him.

Jonathon glared at me. "You're just one big lie, aren't you, Mina?"

He strode across the room to his desk. "You know, Mina,

there are plenty of girls who want to be with me. You think I wanted to waste my time with you?"

I didn't answer.

He picked up his cell phone and held it out to me. "Dial any one of the numbers in my address book. Those girls will tell you that I'm a great guy."

I looked away.

"Who do you think you are?" he spat angrily. "Stuck-up, stupid bitch. You think you can just use me and have me disappear like some lovesick puppy?"

"It wasn't like that," I whispered.

"Then what was it like? Why were you messing with me?" He ran his hands through his hair and turned away from me. "God, Mina. It wasn't like you didn't have a clue. You knew how much I liked you. You've known since the seventh grade."

We both stared down at the floor. I had known for a long time that Jonathon had some kind of crush on me but he was never going to do anything about it. He was just too unsure of himself to try. At least until I started to need his help.

I bit my lower lip to keep it from trembling. What was I doing? How had it gotten so out of control? I couldn't look up at Jonathon, couldn't face his anger, the pain in his face.

"I'm not leaving for another few weeks, Mina," Jonathon said, his head bowed. "I want to see you. Just give me another chance." He raised his head. "I think you owe me that."

I slowly shook my head. "I don't think so, Jonathon."

His upper lip curled slightly. "Damn, Mina. I just want a chance to talk. Look at everything I've done for you. You can't even force yourself to talk to me? Look, I still have to give you the computer program to forge the report cards. I'll get the disk ready and then we can hang out and talk. Okay?"

I swallowed back the bile rising in my throat. I had heard all this before. And every time I relented a little, he asked for more. Of my time, my thoughts. My body. Until. Until I found myself just going along with what he wanted because I didn't know how to ask for his help without giving something in return.

"Okay?" he asked, louder.

"Fine."

I opened the door and walked out.

Alone in the empty hallway, with each step, I feared Jonathon might rush out to follow me, but the only sound in the foyer was the faint music escaping from under Jonathon's closed door.

At the bottom of the stairs, I glanced up at the hallway. The mute statuette of Jesus hung on the wall, his hands clasped together in prayer.

We left before Mrs. Kim had a chance to call down Jonathon to say good-bye. He was packing, I told Uhmma and Mrs. Kim. Uhmma would not hear of us interrupting him again. We left, but not before Mrs. Kim had taken one dark blue suit, ripe with the stench of lobster, out from the hall closet.

suna

Mina and Uhmma walk into the stifling apartment, their clothes limp with sweat, creased with the lines of sitting in the car. Mina walks quickly to their bedroom while Uhmma stands at the door, staring around the apartment, sniffing at the damp ripe odor rising up from the old carpet and second-hand furniture. The lines of her forehead deepen. Uhmma's narrowed eyes come to rest on Suna. And before Uhmma's anger can lash out, find a target for all the miserable heat, Suna runs to her room.

The borrowed dress from the dry cleaners lays crumpled on the floor of their bedroom. They will have to launder it anyway. Mina stands at the dresser in her cutoff shorts and her bra. The drawer with all her shirts is pulled open. Yet, Mina simply stands there, lost in thought, lost in the rectangular patch of night sky framed by their one window. At the sound of Suna closing the door behind her, Mina quickly reaches into the drawer, pulls out a shirt and throws it on.

Mina grabs her CD player and headphones from the top of her bureau and goes to the closet. The sliding door creaks in protest as Mina shoves it open and steps inside, sliding the door shut behind her.

Suna sits alone on her bed and stares out the window. She knows music has always helped Mina find a place other than here. She waits for Mina's voice. The singing is soft at first, but then Mina's voice, like the amber glow of a fire, lights out into the room, deep and burnished. Suna wraps the warmth around her shoulders.

mina

Sometimes when the world felt out of control, when it was all going too fast, or not fast enough, or there was too much yelling about what we didn't have, or Suna had grabbed my hand one too many times that day, I would hide in the closet. Just close the door and sit in the dark. When I was younger, I used to plug my ears and sing quietly, "These are a few of my favorite things," from *The Sound of Music*. Now I put on my earphones and listen to my music.

Sometimes I could listen to the same song over and over again for months. Joni Mitchell, "River." I listened to that for the first half of my junior year. My English teacher was getting a divorce and had it on whenever we walked into her class after lunch. It was also the year when my grades fell. Starting with math. I just couldn't get my head around the proofs. And the more time I spent on math, the less time I had for other subjects. By the time finals came around, I had lost control. I tried to explain to Uhmma, but her way of dealing was to take me straight to Mrs. Kim's house. And Jonathon. If anyone could tutor me, it was perfect, genius Jonathon. What Uhmma failed to understand was that it was too late. My grades had slipped beyond what I needed to get into the best colleges.

All my life Uhmma had held up Harvard as the way to my future. She had told me this myth so many times that I had come to believe it was true. If I couldn't get into Harvard, what was the point? For when you have dreamed and talked about a goal, hoped for so long, anything in comparison did not hold a light.

I focused on Joni's voice. On her heartbreaking cry, that one note trailing off into the sky like a freed balloon. A river. A river that I could skate away on. Just keep skating and never look back. I wish I had a river. That song saved me over and over again. When I thought there was no way out. When I felt disgusted in myself. That song would take me to another place. Until I had something of a plan. All I needed was money. The money that I paid myself from the register was for the start-up costs. For an apartment and food. Just until I could find a job.

I still didn't have an idea of where or how I would live, but I had all my senior year to figure it out. If nothing else, I knew I could always work somewhere punching a cash register. Sometimes, I imagined myself in an empty room: my music is playing and I am dancing. Singing so loud, my neighbors start pounding on the wall. I liked thinking about that. The freedom of it all.

The only thing that still bothered me was leaving Suna

behind. But that would have happened even if I did plan to go to college. Still, I had to figure out a way for Suna to cope with everything. To live with Uhmma without me.

Suna slid open the closet door, letting in a narrow beam of light. She kneeled down and said, "Uhn-nee, it's time for dinner."

The table was set for three. Suna was taking a glass of water over to Apa lying on the couch. Uhmma stood over the stove, ladling hot soup into bowls.

Mina-ya, Uhmma called. Take these to the table. Uhmma handed me the steaming-hot bowls of spicy red je-geh.

Suna-ya, Uhmma called.

Suna was busy helping Apa.

Suna! Uhmma yelled impatiently.

Suna stood up quickly and came to the kitchen.

Uhmma pointed to a cabinet. Get the rice bowls and put the rice on the table.

We moved quickly, silently, until the dinner table was set. Uhmma walked over with the last of the small little dishes of ban-chan to eat with our rice and stew. She inspected the table, making sure everything was properly laid out, before she set the last of our dinner down and then took her place.

Suna and I sat down on either side and put our hands together in prayer.

Uhmma knotted her hands together and brought them up to her chin. She squeezed her eyes tight and rocked to the rhythm of her silent words. Suna and I never really prayed. Simply went through the actions so that we wouldn't get in trouble.

Uhmma opened her eyes and we began our meal.

We ate in silence until I noticed Uhmma watching Suna delicately pick up a tiny floating mushroom and place it on the outer rim of her bowl, along with all the other pieces of mushroom that had been segregated against the white porcelain. Uhmma's eyes began to narrow thinner the longer she watched Suna, who was oblivious to everything except her mushrooms.

Uhmma, I said quickly, I signed up for my SAT prep class.

Uhmma turned toward me. Good, she said. She took a sip of her soup and began her questioning.

How many people are in the class? The library was offering it for free?

I nodded.

Uhmma smiled and said, Mrs. Kim always knows these things. Did I not tell you that she knows these things? Tomorrow she is going to send someone to help us. What would we do without Mrs. Kim? Uhmma shook her head. She took a sip of her soup and then asked, When are you getting college catalogs? Mrs. Kim said that Jonathon started to get catalogs right away after he took his SATs the first time. Did you have a good conversation with him this evening? Did you make sure to ask him all about his application process?

Yes. I nodded and took a sip of my hot stew. My face was coated in sweat.

Uhmma continued, We must find him a nice gift for helping you so much. He has been such a good older brother to you. Mrs. Kim said that when he found out that you were coming over, he canceled his trip to the beach.

I could feel Uhmma's eyes on me. Uhmma leaned forward.

Mina, she said, her eyes focused and sharp, you are conducting yourself like a good girl.

I made a point of staring back at her, my eyes hard and edged with indignation as the blood pounded in my ears. Don't worry, Uhmma, I said.

Uhmma's face relaxed. She continued, You have worked too hard to make your life a mess. You have your entire future ahead of you. Anything you want, you can have. You just have to remember to work hard and remain focused. Uhmma reached over and brushed a trickle of sweat off my temple. She smiled at me.

My beautiful daughter, Uhmma said. I am so proud of you. She sighed softly and glanced over at the couch. I wish, she continued, that I could have done more for you. I wish we had the money to send you to that expensive preparation class.

I looked up at Uhmma's face every once in a while as she spoke more to herself than to me. It always seemed that in wanting the world for me, she always returned to what we did not have in our lives. In her life. For her life had not always been this way. She had come from a respectable family. A wealthy family, she had said. She was accustomed to better things. Deserved better things. If only Apa had seen fit to make more of himself instead of relying on the back of his youthful wife.

I listened to Uhmma droning on and focused my attention on the mole at the tail end of Uhmma's left eyebrow. It was an ugly thing. When Suna and I were younger, we used to pretend to be Uhmma by sticking gum above our eyebrow. I couldn't understand how others could think Uhmma beautiful, but how many times had I heard various church members remark to me on how fortunate I was to have such a lovely mother. So young too, they added, right before they stepped away, glancing over at Apa huddled in his chair.

Uhmma paused in midslurp of her stew. Mina, Uhmma said. Mina, are you listening to me?

Yes, Uhmma, I said and buried my head deeper into my bowl of je-geh.

Then what did I just ask you to do?

I held still. Probably something ridiculous, I thought and took another sip of my stew, the red chili oil coating the back of my spoon, my lips. Something as ridiculous as making us eat this hot stew that was supposed to make us somehow cooler in this ridiculous heat.

I felt Suna glance up from her task, her eyes studying my face.

What did I just say, Uhmma asked again.

I stared at Uhmma sideways. Directed my answer to her mole. I do not remember.

You were not listening, Uhmma said, leaning forward.

"Whatever," I mumbled under my breath.

Do I have to remind you how much I have had to sacrifice? Uhmma asked over her bowl, her words and the steam mingling into a fiery breath. All of it for you! Everything I do is for your benefit and you treat me as though I were some maid. Here to serve you. Who makes your food, makes sure you have enough clothes to wear? Who makes sure you have all the books you need? Who has to handle all the responsibilities at the cleaners? Uhmma paused, turned her head to the side, took in a breath to continue her tirade, only her eyes fell upon Suna.

Suna, who sat frozen in her seat, every line in her body rigid and tense. Except for her hand. Like a toy doll with only one function, she moved her chopsticks through the stew, fishing out each and every piece of mushroom. Her concentration, her need to cleanse from her bowl all that was wrong blinded her to the hand. Uhmma's hand. A white claw slashed through the air and smashed against the side of the bowl.

The crimson bolt stained the collar of Suna's shirt, traveled along the crease of her nose, ran down her neck.

Uhmma slouched over the table, pressing the heels of her hands into her eyes.

Why do you have to make it so hard? Uhmma asked.

suna

Suna kicks the sheets off the bed and lies perfectly still, willing a breeze to float over her body. She hears the light rhythmic breathing of Mina sleeping in the bed across from her. There is faint pulsing heat at the base of her neck from where the hot stew splashed her. She gingerly touches her skin, pressing down lightly. If only she could tell her mother that she had been listening. To the stories and descriptions that had been told so many times, she had memorized them by heart. Like fairy tales. Suna loves to imagine that someday her grandparents will come and save her family. Finally give her mother the life she has always wanted. This is a recurring fantasy that Suna likes to play with in her mind. As though unlocking a forbidden box. She secretly opens the box when no one is looking, when she needs to pretend that everything will be better. Sitting at the dinner table, picking out the mushrooms from her soup, she imagined her grandparents in Korea eating mushrooms like her mother. Such earthy, slimy things. She remembers learning about them in science. How they are called fungus and like to grow in dark, damp places. Like a festering secret. She stares up at the ceiling and imagines her grandparents walking into the apartment, their arms loaded with gifts.

Uhmma's face, as though appearing from a dream, steps into the room, a white washcloth in her hand. She steps quickly, quietly across the room and comes to sit on Suna's bed. Uhmma brings her finger to her lips and then points to Mina sleeping. Suna nods. Uhmma gently places the cool wet washcloth on Suna's burn, patting it in place with the palm of her hand. The dark puffy skin around Uhmma's eyes makes her look tired. Old.

Before Suna can reach for her, Uhmma is gone. Across the room, quietly closing the door behind her. And when Suna blinks, she believes for a moment that it must have been a dream. A ghost. Except for the cool weight of the washcloth on her chest. Suna falls asleep holding the cloth as though it were her heart.

mina

*I*t was the sound of his voice that I heard first. Slow, raspy, the softest lilt on certain consonants. Suna and I stood near the back door of the dry cleaners, looking at each other, our eyebrows raised, wondering who was inside with Uhmma and Apa. We walked toward the voices near the pressing machines.

"This one. Some time." Apa struggled to find the right English word. "Yes. Stuck. Stuck. Pull down like this."

Uhmma stood off to one side, a hand at her waist. We came to stand next to her. Apa and a young man were bent over, fixing the shirt press. They straightened up as we approached.

"Moon," Suna blurted out and then clamped her hand over her mouth, shaking her head as though she too understood she had momentarily lost her mind.

He was taller than Apa, but he wasn't so tall that Apa had to tilt his head back to look into his eyes. The baseball cap that he wore, the brim casting a shadow over his eyes, was faded and worn, the Padres logo barely visible. For a second I tried to place him at my school, but the way he returned my gaze before lowering his eyes, the slightest show of stubble on his chin and upper lip, the dark tan along his neck and fore-arms, I knew there was no way he was in school now.

Apa waved us over. Mina-ya, Suna-ya, come here.

Uhmma blocked our path. No, she said, they do not need to meet him.

Yuhbow, Apa said, they will have to work with him.

Apa gestured to us. "My daugh-tors."

"Hi," he said and held out his hand, his eyes cast down-ward.

"He name, Is . . . Is . . ."

"Ysrael," he said and smiled at Apa, his eyes glancing up briefly from the floor.

"Yes-rail," Apa repeated to himself. "Yes-rail."

"Hi," I said and shook his hand. I quickly let his hand go after finding his skin soft and cool. I knew my own palms were sweaty and warm. I felt Suna's presence behind me. I stepped out of the way. "This is my sister, Suna."

Suna stood there frozen for a moment before she darted back behind me. Ysrael leaned to the right and waved to her, his eyes finally leaving the floor. When he smiled, the dimples along the sides of his lips were long and elegant, stretching from his cheeks to his chin. Except where they joined the scar at his jawline. The white indented scar, a half circle, like a bite into an apple, was just to the right of his chin.

Uhmma watched all this with a tight, fake smile on her face. That is enough, she interrupted in Korean. Mina, go watch the front of the store.

Ysrael tilted his head as Uhmma spoke. I could see him trying to puzzle out what had been said.

Suna and I reluctantly walked away, but not before glancing over our shoulders again to catch another look at Ysrael.

Uhmma came up front with us, muttering, Mrs. Kim said that she would send someone. She did not say that she would send a Mexican. I must call her right away. This has to be a mistake.

Uhmma put on her fake voice for the phone. She spoke brightly, Mrs. Kim. She paused and frowned as she listened.

Yes, she said. He is here. Are you sure he is the right person? Uhmma bit down on the fleshly pad of her thumb as she listened. Her voice returned to normal. Yes, of course. Another Korean would have been far too expensive for us. Yes, I see. Thank you very much, Mrs. Kim. Thank you. Uhmma carefully placed the phone down, her eyes cast away from us.

In the back, Apa in his broken English was trying to explain all the various stain removers to Ysrael. Uhmma went to go find them.

Suna's father, she interrupted in Korean. He cannot do that properly. He will not know the difference between all the stains. Look at him. He can barely keep himself clean.

Yuhbow, Apa argued weakly, he can do this work.

Uhmma raised her voice. *No.* You want us to lose our business. You are as big an idiot as he is. I will handle this.

Apa said, "My wife. She do this."

"Are you sure?" Ysrael asked. "There's a lot of clothes here."

Uhmma answered Ysrael, "You go do shirts now."

I heard two sets of footsteps coming to the front. I quickly pulled out my SAT books and pretended to be busy.

Suna's father, Uhmma called out. Come here.

One set of footsteps went back. The other set continued forward to the presses. The steady sound of the foot pedal and steam releasing started up.

Uhmma yelled at Apa in the back of the store. She said, You must keep your eyes on him. Some of these young Mexicans steal and then they disappear. Mrs. Kim told me about their dishwasher at the restaurant who ran away with all the register money.

I turned my page with a clear snap, gripping my pencil in disgust. I wondered what Mrs. Kim would think if she saw the brand-new leather jacket her perfect Stanford-bound son had hanging in his locker, the one thing that he never took home. Jonathon had let that poor dishwasher hang out to dry when Mrs. Kim checked the books and noticed money missing. That was how Jonathon learned never to take too much from the register at one time.

Yuhbow, Apa argued, he will not steal from us. He seems like a nice young man. Let us just try. Besides, in a week or two, I will be able to work again.

Uhmma did not answer. After a long silence, Apa's slow footsteps walked back to the office.

By midafternoon, in between the lunch-hour rush of errands being completed and before everyone got off work, there was a haze of heat outside so thick, it looked like fog. I stood by the register and wondered where Suna had been all morning.

She had stayed close to me for a while, trying to help with the tags and hanging up the clothes, until one time I turned to give her a coat to hang up, and she had simply disappeared. Apa most likely was still in the office, dozing with the fan aimed at his head. And the presses were silent.

I walked back to the office to check and see if Suna was there. I stretched out to look past some clothes at the back door but saw only the faint profile of Uhmma taking her cigarette break. She sat on an overturned bucket just outside the back doorway, her body in the shade of the building, the cigarette smoke streaming behind her into the store. As I turned to go to the office, I saw him out of the corner of my eye. He was washing his hands at one of the large sinks, letting the water slowly trickle over his hands as he read the labels of the various stain removers that we kept on a shelf. I thought about trying to talk to him. Tell him to ignore Uhmma, that she was always like that. Ask him if the presses worked smoothly. That sometimes you had to clean the foot pedal 'cause it got gunked up. And as I tried on all these sentences, testing each one, he turned around. A smile jumped to my face in a reflex of fear and surprise. Ysrael's eyes immediately darted to the floor, but he smiled and nodded his head slightly. He turned back around to turn off the water, and in that moment, I ran. Safely behind the office door, I stood waiting, listening for any sound that he had followed.

suna

*S*una cannot help but follow him. Not so close that he might notice her, or so she thinks, but at a distance, behind plastic-shrouded clothes and noisy machines. She feels a claim to him, that somehow Ysrael belongs to her. Because she had seen him first. He is still Moon in her mind.

His profile flickers in and out of focus as she moves closer and closer, unable to resist studying his face, his movements. There are razor-thin, long scars along his jaw that she had not noticed before. And the deep well of his moon scar is more jagged and angry than she remembered. She wonders about the story behind that mark. She can see a bit of his thick black hair tucked behind his ears, but the rest is hidden under his baseball cap.

She crouches down low and watches him work the presses, rhythmically steaming each dress pant so they are left with perfect center creases. Apa can never stand the heat for long and often takes breaks, leaving Suna to try her hand at creating those crisp straight lines. But Suna will misalign the pants, try to reline them, steam them again and again and find them smelling sweet and smoky, cast with a peculiar iridescent sheen that Uhmma will inevitably find and scream at her for burning the clothes. Ysrael does not make mistakes. He works steadily, his eyes fixed on each pair of pants, his hands quickly smoothing out each pant leg before lowering the press. His hands are lean and long and every time he waits for the press to do its magic, he puts his right hand on top of the handle, thumb and forefinger pinched together, strumming the air. And above the din of machines churning, the register clicking, steam sighing, Suna believes she can hear the faintest sounds of his music.

mina

*H*e did not say much. Always started the morning with a hello and a nod to everyone and then slipped behind the press or sat down to pull plastic wrappers over the clothes. Sometimes if we were in the same area at the same time he might smile, his eyes flickering up to my face before they rested somewhere on the floor, and softly say, "Hey." He had a way of making himself disappear, and though the presses continued hissing, sometimes it was easy to forget that he was around.

I filled in a bubble on my practice test, my hand moving in time to the music that was playing on my CD player. Vocabulary words were straightforward. I could handle that. And though I should have been working on the math section, I chose to avoid it. I filled in a few more vocabulary word bubbles and then checked my answers in the back. I caught my breath.

Jonathon's writing, bold, evenly slanted to the right, was all along the edges in the back. I closed the book and turned up the volume on my player. I didn't know why I was even bothering. It wasn't like the SATs were going to change anything. Even if I got a perfect score, my GPA would bring me down. The best I could hope for was a state school. But that just wouldn't be good enough. Not for Uhmma. I blew out my breath. Since the fourth grade, when the school placed me in the upper track and my teacher told Uhmma that I had potential, Uhmma had been making plans for me. And it all hinged on the best college. Which led to the best job and husband. The best family. The best life. As much as I hated Uhmma for all the pressure she put on me, for all the times she bragged and held me out like some show pony, as much as I wanted to scream at her, I couldn't. Because I knew how she had sacrificed for me.

I caught her once, soon after Suna was born. Instead of shooing me away like all the other times, she had held out a small photo.

You resemble him more than me, she said and smiled through her tears.

I studied the grainy black-and-white photo. He was sitting in a chair, dressed in a suit as though going to work in one of those office buildings downtown. The smooth skin of his face made him look almost like a boy. A handsome boy pretending to be a man. Uhmma pulled me into her lap.

You must never tell anyone, Uhmma whispered. Even then, as young as I had been, I knew this was our secret.

Who is he? I asked.

Uhmma rocked me in her lap and stared out the window. Someone I loved, she whispered.

I asked, Where did he go? Is he coming back?

Uhmma shook her head. He was not allowed.

I patted her cheeks to make her look at me.

Uhmma pressed her lips together and held me firmly by the shoulders. Her voice hardened. Mina, I do not want to hear you talking about him to anyone. Not even your father. Not one word. She pointed her finger at me. Do you understand?

I nodded.

She pulled me back against her chest. Held me so hard, I had to take small sips of air. She nuzzled my neck, breathed in the scent of my hair. She whispered, How could I have given you up. My beautiful daughter. You are all I have left of him.

We never spoke of him again. When I asked later to look at his photo, a strange grimace settled over her face and she pushed me away, told me there was no such thing. For a long time, I believed he was some kind of uncle. A part of Uhmma's family. The family we were not supposed to talk about. The family that we had left behind to come to America. For a long time, I did not understand. Then slowly, like a stain that spreads, its edges growing wider, fuller, my suspicions grew. The point at which I started wondering if he was my father was never very clear. Thinking back to it was like looking back at the change in my body. It didn't happen overnight. It just crept up on me. When Uhmma tore into

Apa for the things he could not help, when Apa bowed his head in defeat, I sensed that stranger passing by.

As much as I wanted to tell Jonathon that it was over, that I didn't need his help, I couldn't face the disappointment in Uhmma's eyes. The way she would look at me afterward, knowing that all she had worked for, sacrificed, all of it for nothing.

I knew I had to meet Jonathon before he left. I needed the program for the report cards and then it would be over. He would be gone and I would have all of my senior year to save up more money. After that? Maybe when I was finally away from her, I would tell her the truth. Maybe when I did not have to live with her frustration every day, see it settle into her body in angry, resentful folds, the way it did with Suna and Apa. Maybe then.

Someone coughed behind me. I whipped around. Ysrael held up a pressed shirt, a rush job that I had asked him to do just an hour before. For once, his eyes weren't cast down, but up at me.

"Oh, yeah," I muttered, unable to meet his eyes. Though I knew he couldn't have read my mind, the thought that he had been watching me made my toes curl in embarrassment. I tried to remember what exactly I had been doing, how I had been standing. I tried to look busy by pushing the key on the cash register that displayed the time. I could feel him just standing there. Behind me. Waiting. What did he want?

Sometimes there are these moments that linger in the mind. They are never explainable. Why that time and not others. Why that look and not others. They just exist. I turned around and there he was. Standing perfectly still. The sunlight slanting across his lips, his chin, his scar. Illuminating all that was flawed. His dark brown eyes studying my hair. He waited so patiently, without judgment, without anger, just stood there with that white shirt held out in front of him like a flag. And in that moment, in that terrible heat, I wanted to tell him everything. Let the weight of my lies slide off my shoulders. But all I could do was take the shirt and whisper, "Thank you."

The free SAT sessions at the library started at 7:00 P.M., but Uhmma made sure we were out the door of the apartment by 6:30 even though we lived five minutes from the library. She handed me Suna's heavy backpack full of books to return.

Make sure you get a seat up front, Uhmma said to me.

I nodded and waited for Suna to finish tying her laces. I dreaded sitting there while we practiced drill after drill. At least Suna would have time to wander around and get some reading done.

We parked around the side of the brick building because the lot in front was completely full. The central library was almost always teeming with people. And with the heat so bad, the inside nice and air-conditioned, it was busier than normal. A large group of kids sat on the cement steps, talking. Suna and I walked wordlessly by them. Most were from the middle school that Suna would be attending this fall and I could tell that Suna was studying them closely, staring at their faces, the girls' thin-strapped tank tops and tight hip-hugging jeans. One of the smoking girls caught Suna's look and asked, "What you looking at?"

Suna bit her lip.

"Come on," I said and gently pushed her toward the glass doors.

Once inside, Suna moved quickly toward the children's room, not even glancing over to the teen center where most of the kids her age were sitting on top of tables, in front of computers, whispering to each other.

I stopped by the front desk to ask the librarian what time the prep session would be over and then made my way to the children's room to tell Suna.

The children's section was empty. The puppet and story time corner deserted except for a few stray hand puppets carelessly tossed on the rug. I knew Suna was probably sitting on the floor somewhere, her head turned sideways so that she could read the titles. She was rereading all the C. S. Lewis books again. I saw a shadow sitting on the floor and turned to head down the aisle.

He was on the floor, reading a book. I froze when I realized who it was. Ysrael glanced up to see who was approaching. His voice was pitched high with surprise. "Hey."

I clutched my SAT books to my chest and waved awkwardly. What was he doing at the library? In the children's section?

"You finding what you're looking for?" he asked, sounding like a librarian.

I pointed to my notebook. "I have an SAT prep class."

Ysrael raised one eyebrow.

I took a deep breath. "They have it here Mondays and Wednesdays."

He nodded and smiled. "Your mom makes you study pretty hard, huh?"

It was my turn to nod.

We searched for other things to say, and when the moment grew long and tense with anticipation, we turned to study the books on the shelves.

"I better get to my—"

"Why don't you sit—"

We tried not to smile at each other.

Ysrael pointed to the books. "I used to come here all the time when I was a kid. I remembered how quiet it was. I don't really read these books anymore."

I laughed, my voice echoing through the empty room. "You mean *The Little Princess* isn't your favorite book?"

He shrugged. "Well, just my second favorite. I mean after"—he leaned forward to read the spines of the books sitting on the shelf directly across from him—"*Encyclopedia Brown.*"

"Hey, that's my favorite!"

"See, I knew we had a connection."

I blushed and glanced down at my notebook.

"Sit down?" he asked.

I bit my bottom lip and slowly lowered myself to the ground, sitting cross-legged, a few feet from him. "I have to go soon."

He checked his watch. "What time is the class?"

"Seven."

"Cool. We have approximately ten minutes to share our life stories."

I snorted. "I can sum up mine in two."

Ysrael absentmindedly ran the knuckles of his hand along his jaw. "Yeah, mine doesn't seem all that complicated either. I mean, what's there to say about work, work and more work. Right?" He grinned.

"Hey." I mockingly tried to look hurt. "You don't have glowing words about ironing shirts and pressing pants? Come on, you're supposed to try and flatter the daughter of your boss."

"More like try and get on the good side of your mom."

I studied the books again.

"Sorry." Ysrael leaned forward. "Sometimes my mouth says stuff before my brain kicks in. I mean, your mom isn't that bad. She's just really serious and—"

"Cruel," I finished for him.

Ysrael shrugged.

I smiled. "My dad likes you, though, and that's what counts."

"I like your pops. He's a good guy. Too bad about his back. Has it always been like that?"

"Yeah. It gets bad off and on."

"Yeah, my brother-in-law threw out his back when he was working the grape fields in Napa."

"Napa? Is that around here?"

He lowered his eyes, the black dust of his lashes a shadow against the brown of his cheeks. "It's up near San Francisco.

In this valley with all these hills and green trees. Man, it's so beautiful up there. When the sun rises and hits the fields, the grapes start shining this soft dusty purple." He drew up his knees. "And San Francisco looks like this city that just popped out of the ocean. It kind of hangs there on the edge."

"Is that where you're from?" I asked.

He shook his head. "Nah, I just went up there to visit my sis. I'm moving up there at the end of the summer. As soon as I get my money together to find myself a place."

"Can't you stay with your sister?"

Ysrael studied the books in front of him again. "It's not that easy. They move around a lot and there's not that much room."

I nodded as though I understood.

Ysrael checked his watch. "Shoot, I made you late. Damn, me and my mouth."

"It's okay," I said. "I didn't want to go anyway. It's useless, but my mom wanted me to try and raise my scores."

"There's nothing wrong with trying. I wish I had tried harder at school. You better get going. I'm taking off for the beach anyway."

I pretended one of my legs had fallen asleep and pounded it with my fist. "You going to meet some friends at the beach?"

"Nah, I just go to practice my guitar. It's nice to be near the waves." He laughed. "That way the ocean can drown out my bad playing." He stood up, stretching his legs, shaking one and then the other. I stood up with him, glancing at the book in his hand. *Songwriting for Beginners.* He saw my look and moved the book to his side.

"Have a good class," Ysrael said, quickly meeting my eyes before he looked away.

"Thanks," I answered. I turned around to leave, but then turned back.

"Can you tell Suna that I'll be done at nine o'clock?"

"Suna's here?" Ysrael asked.

I smiled. "Yeah, she's hidden somewhere in one of these aisles."

"No problem," he said.

suna

Suna sits cross-legged on the floor, an open book in her lap, her hands playing with the laces of her shoes as she reads. A shadow blocks her light. She looks up. Ysrael stands in front of her with a smile on his face, so much like the first time she saw him, but this time she smiles in return. His lips move in a soft hush as he crouches down next to her. She turns away from him, reaching quickly into the back pocket of her shorts and then up to her ear.

He watches her furtive movements with a wrinkled brow, the way she drops her chin and moves her hair aside, fitting a white contraption over her ear. With her fingers, she combs a section of her hair back over her ear.

She lifts her face and finds him studying her. The corners of his lips turned down ever so slightly. He gently reaches out and touches her hair, tucks it behind her ear, exposing the hard white contraption. His eyes grow wide in understanding. She shakes her head, smoothing her hair back over her ear.

Ysrael draws his knuckles along the length of his jaw, along the deep groove of his scar. He presses his thumb into the scar and looks away. Down the aisle. He returns his gaze to Suna, his eyes clouded and shiny.

Suna studies his face, wonders where he has gone. What memory called up the tenderness in his eyes.

Ysrael reaches for her hand and stands up. "Come on. Let's go to the beach."

mina

Where was Suna? I was going to kill her. I checked my watch. The librarian behind me cleared her throat again.

"Could I just check upstairs before you close?"

She pushed her cart out from behind her desk and said, "Go ahead. I didn't see anyone up there, though, when I checked. Are you sure she knew to wait for you here?"

I nodded, my anger starting to give way to fear. I ran up the stairs, taking the steps two at a time. Where could she be? I checked all the aisles again. Could someone have taken her? She wasn't one to talk to strangers, but maybe someone from school? Her only real friend at school had moved away the past summer and her friend from church was over an hour away. I shook my head. There wasn't anyone. She would have waited for me.

"She's not up there?" the librarian asked as I headed toward the front doors.

"No. She must have gone home." I pushed back the glass

doors, stepping into the hot dry night. I stood on the front steps, clutching my books to my chest. Maybe she did go home. She must be at home. I tried to picture her in our room, but all I could see was Uhmma standing there, one hand on her hip, questioning Suna as she stepped into the house by herself. A film of sickness coated my mouth. Where was she?

A car with a broken headlight turned into the parking lot and stopped before the steps. Ysrael quickly got out of the driver's seat. Suna stepped out of the passenger's side more slowly.

"Hey," Ysrael called as he bounded up the steps. "Sorry we're so late," he said, trying to catch his breath. "There was an accident on 805 and—"

Suna smiled and waved as she walked up the steps. "Yeah, sorry we were late, Uhn-nee."

I pressed my lips together, took a deep breath and ignored them both as I walked down the steps and got into my car. Suna jumped in just as I pressed on the gas and screeched out of the parking lot.

I refused to speak to her. At night I felt Suna's eyes on my back, her plaintive questions aimed at my still figure in the dark.

"Why are you so mad at me? What did I do?"

Her questions went unanswered until they sank into deep sighs. And even when my anger had passed, I couldn't bring myself to talk to her. How could I explain the feeling of being the one left behind? That he had chosen to take her over me? It was a role that Suna knew too well. I was ashamed to find myself pouting like a child.

Uhmma continued to ignore Ysrael, yet monitored every piece of clothing he touched. He never said anything when she suddenly barged into his space to check on a shirt or a dress that he was pressing. He simply stepped out of the way until she left satisfied, or he stood quietly nodding his head as she ranted at the piece of clothing in her hand. He seemed not to mind her flares of temper, her angry silences and moody stances by the back door, smoking her cigarette. And maybe this was why he got along so well with Apa. The two of them, one straight back, one slightly crooked, heading to lunch at the fried chicken place at the end of the strip mall.

I didn't want to think about whether Ysrael would be at the library again. Yet, as I scanned the clothes in my closet that night, I worried about what looked good. Suna sat on the edge of her bed, silently watching me move around the room.

"He's going to be there," she whispered.

I whirled around, holding a shirt in my hand. "What are you talking about? How do you know that?"

She shrugged her shoulders.

"Then you shouldn't talk about things you don't know," I said and angrily pulled the shirt over my head.

Suna hugged her dog to her chest. "He'll be there."

I ignored her comment and picked up my prep books. "Come on," I said, walking out of the room. "Hurry up or you're gonna make me late."

Ysrael sat on the steps of the library a few feet from the usual gang that hung out in front. He stood up and walked over as soon as he saw our car pull into the parking lot. I slowed down and stopped beside him.

"Hey," he said, leaning into the open window. "Prep class, right?"

I nodded.

I stared stone-faced, forward, speaking to the windshield. "She didn't have permission to go. You should have asked me first."

Ysrael nodded. "I know."

A car behind us honked. I motioned for him to meet us along the side of the library and pulled forward.

"Uhn-nee." Suna touched my arm.

I jerked back my arm. "Well, you should have told me. You should have asked."

Ysrael appeared at my window again. "Hey," he said softly. "I'm sorry. I didn't mean to cause any trouble. I just thought it would be nicer for Suna to hang at the beach instead of at the library."

I ignored them. Took the keys out of the ignition. I reached for my books on the backseat.

"Mina," Ysrael said. "Mina."

The sound of my name. His voice scratchy and crackling of old records.

Ask me, I thought fiercely. Ask me.

He turned away, his eyes resting on the distant brick wall of the library. "I wish you could come with me," he said.

I sat back in my seat, let the weight of his words settle in my body. "I can."

Ysrael frowned. "Hold on. What about class? What are

you going to tell your mom? SATs aren't something you can just take over whenever you want."

I laughed. "Jesus, you sound like my mom. The class sucks, by the way. And"—I waved my prep books—"I have all this Princeton Review stuff from this guy I know."

Ysrael rubbed the side of his jaw with his knuckles. "I don't want to get you in trouble. You sure?"

I had never been more. *"Yes!"*

He slowly grinned. "My car or yours?"

We drove in the Sentra. Old as it was, Sally was still looking better than Ysrael's cousin's beat-up Ford. Suna sat in the back but kept leaning forward to hear what we were saying.

"How long have you had this car?" Ysrael asked, checking out the mileage as we sped down the freeway.

I grinned. "Pretty old, huh. I can't believe it still runs."

"Sally just needs to be loved. If you rub her dash, she really gets going," Suna added.

"Sally?" Ysrael said.

"That's her name," Suna said. "Sally Sentra, the lean, mean fightin' machine."

Ysrael laughed. "You'll have to name the Ford so it'll run better."

We spilled out of Sally and onto the beach with various rhythms popping from our lips. "Frankie Ford farts all over his doors." "Frances Ford can do many chores."

The sound of the waves breaking along the beach turned our attention to the sea. I breathed in deeply, letting the cool ocean air wash me clean. Suna came and stood next to me. All my earlier anger seemed so childish and extreme. I reached out and caught Suna's hand, giving it a squeeze. She smiled and swung our hands high into the air.

Ysrael joined us, his hands shoved deep into his back pockets, shoulders high and near his ears as though he were cold. "It's beautiful here," he said, meeting my eyes.

I nodded in agreement. Suna let go of my hand and walked out in front, heading for the sand. I stood in my place, unsure of whether to follow Suna or to wait for Ysrael.

"Go ahead. I just have to get my guitar from the car," Ysrael said.

I chased after Suna, the giddiness of being away from everything—Uhmma's expectations, studying for the SATs, the dry cleaners—infecting me until I felt three years old again.

We ran for the water's edge, hurrying to kick off our shoes before the waves ate up our feet. I jokingly made to push Suna in and she screamed and tried to push me back. We jostled back and forth, kicking up the water, the last rays of the dying sun glowing on our faces, our hands, our shoulders.

"Look, Uhn-nee," Suna said and splashed water toward the horizon. "Sundrops." The sunset rays caught each bead of water suspended in the air, if only for a moment, and shaped them into jewels. I placed my arm around her shoulders and hugged her close. This sister of mine.

The soft distant notes of music caught my ears and we leaned into the sound, heading up the beach toward Ysrael.

suna

*Y*srael plays with his eyes intense on the strings. Mina turns away slightly, as though to give him privacy. The music at first is hard to hear over the waves. Suna concentrates, focuses on the notes, on the way Ysrael lets the people who walk by, families, teenagers, a baby, sway the music until it seems that each body moves in time to the song.

Suna buries her hands in the sand and closes her eyes, lets Ysrael's playing take her to another place. Out to the sea. On a boat bobbing along the waters, sails billowing, hair whipped back, the sun so bright, it hurts to smile. And when Ysrael begins to sing, his voice at first low and raspy at the edges, Suna bows her head and a breeze washes down the back of her neck. He strums loudly and lets his voice open, throws it to the sky as though it were a bird. The note flies up. Alone. Perfect.

Ysrael softens his playing, lets the last few notes speak to each other in a private conversation. Back and forth. Back and forth. Silence.

Suna opens her eyes. Ysrael huddles over his guitar and goes through the notes, tightening the strings here and there. Mina sits with her legs drawn up, her arms wrapped around her knees, her eyes gazing out at the sea. A look of pain echoes across her face and she begins to methodically chew her bottom lip. Suna stares at her for a moment. She has seen this look before. Her sister grappling with a ghost, a haunting that will not leave her be. This look, this one part of Mina's life, Suna is not allowed to know. Suna stands up and goes to gather seashells for Mina.

mina

Υsrael's playing held such a longing. To be in this world, to hold on to this life. He played with his heart. And where was mine? I stared out at the sea. I had buried it so long ago. Buried it under all of Uhmma's dreams for me. Buried it under all the lies I told to live up to those expectations. When had what Uhmma wanted become more important than what I wanted? Did I even know what that was anymore?

Ysrael came over and sat down next to me, placing his guitar on the sand. I smiled, a weak tug at the corners. "That was great."

Ysrael looked doubtful. "You look sad. Did I do that?"

I smiled wider. "No. No. It wasn't your playing. Well, kind of. It just made me think about things."

Ysrael nodded and buried his feet into the sand. "I guess that's good."

We sat in silence, watching Suna off in the distance gather

seashells. Ysrael cleared his throat. "Has she always worn a hearing aid?"

"Yeah," I said. "Since she was a baby."

"That's too bad."

"It's actually okay. She's got some hearing in one ear and her hearing aid for the bad ear. But it's getting her to wear the aid that's hard. She likes to escape, which drives my mom crazy."

Ysrael glanced over at me. "Does your mom give Suna a hard time about it?"

I tilted my head to one side, thinking about a way to explain. "It's what she doesn't give Suna."

Ysrael scooped up a handful of sand and let the grains trickle out between his fingers. "Like she gave up on her," he said.

I nodded. "Suna will always somehow be damaged."

Ysrael pulled the guitar onto his lap and played with the strings for a second, his eyes tight at the corners. "I know that feeling. I didn't realize she wore a hearing aid until I saw her at the library that last time. I guess I just wanted to do something for her that would make her smile."

I nodded. I stared at him, wondering about his history, about the scar on his face. And because he had shared so much already, had given a piece of himself over in his music, I asked, "How did you get that scar?"

He touched it for a second with the back of his knuckles. "How long have you guys owned that dry cleaning business?" he asked as though he hadn't heard my question.

"Five years," I said, focusing on burying my hands in the sand. I should have never asked.

"Yeah, that's a long time," he said.

I glanced over at him. I longed for the words that would take us back to the beginning.

"I'm sorry," I said to his stooped back.

Ysrael stood up without responding. He picked up his guitar. In a graceful arc, he swung it up over his head, letting the strap fall across his chest and shoulder. The guitar nestled along the curve of his back. He walked forward a few steps and then turned back, waiting for me.

We walked silently toward the water's edge. Suna was crouched in the distance, at the edge of the shoreline, digging her hands into the wet sand. Her head was bowed in concentration and though I waved, she did not look up.

Ysrael clasped his hands behind his neck and rocked back on his heels, anticipating the ocean crash against his ankles. I hooked my thumbs in the front pocket of my shorts and tried not to sway as the wave hit my shins. I spoke to my wiggling toes.

"I used to hate the beach when I was little," I said. I could feel Ysrael looking at me. "I thought the sand made the world too tipsy."

Ysrael laughed. A clear, shining, one-note bark that broke with the sea. "And now?" he asked.

I turned to him. "I feel like I can breathe again."

Ysrael stared at the horizon and nodded silently. We stayed that way, not speaking, not moving, just let the sea lap around us. The sun had dipped below the horizon, but the sky still held on to the memory of the light. The brilliant colors balanced on the crests of the waves.

"It happened when I was a baby," he said. "Back home. In Mexico. My mama says I had just started walking, getting into trouble when she wasn't looking."

He paused, cut his eyes to me before looking back at the sea, buried his hands into his back pockets. "There was this pig. Mean as hell. I remember how my brothers and I used to poke at it to see him get angry. Stupid what we do as kids."

I reached out to tell him that he didn't have to tell me anything. That whatever had happened to him was in the past. And yet, I couldn't bring myself to touch him.

"They had to kill it before it could kill me. I don't remember anything about the attack except sitting on the fence." He turned to me. I tried not to stare at his scar, keeping my eyes on his eyes.

"Kids used to come from all over, chase me down to try and touch my face for good luck. 'Cause I survived. 'Cause I was some freak with half my face bitten off. A walking miracle, looking like that. I wore a bandage, but that didn't stop the kids who just wanted to scare themselves. See if what was under the cover was worse than what they had imagined. Worse than what they had heard from other kids."

Ysrael smiled. "I got to be really fast running away from all the teasing. Not even the adults could catch me. Then this relief organization from the U.S. came looking for me. They had heard about the pig boy even in Mexico City." He shook his head. "They're so arrogant, these American doctors. They think they can fix the world. They took me to L.A. and a couple of operations later, they sent me back to Mexico City to show off their handiwork. The newspapers said it was the best modern medicine had to offer." He jutted out his chin at me. "What do you think?"

The harshness and anger in his voice forced me to step back. Ysrael immediately lowered his chin. "What did they expect? That closing the hole in my face would make my life better?" Ysrael closed his eyes. "You know, I was happy when I first saw the doctors. I thought they had come to help us 'cause my mama was sick. But it wasn't her they wanted to see. They wanted me. I tried to tell them that my mother needed the doctors more. But they kept saying they weren't the right doctors for that kind of sickness. They couldn't do anything about her stomach."

Ysrael stated quietly, "She was in so much pain at the end. Where was the best of medicine then?"

He told me how he left Mexico with his older sister and her husband, leaving their father behind in that small village, traveling with a guide, a coyote, for a week before they finally landed in San Diego, half dead to the world. "These scars are nothing compared to what it looked like," he said, raking his knuckles along his jaw. He pressed his thumb into the crescent moon of his scar. "I'm nothing like what I used to be."

The library parking lot was dark and nearly empty except for a few cars when we returned from the beach. I slowed down and pulled into the parking space next to his Ford. I turned off the engine and sat silently, gripping the steering wheel with both hands. Suna stirred in the back, a soft snoring coming from the corner.

"Are we okay?" he asked.

"What do you mean?" I said.

The outline of his profile turned to me. "I didn't mean to scare you."

"You didn't."

"You sure?" he asked.

"I wanted to know," I said.

"See what you get for being nosy," he said.

I smiled. I could see the flash of whiteness from his teeth.

Ysrael opened the car door and turned to leave. "See you tomorrow," he said.

I nodded. "See you."

I drove home thinking about Ysrael's story. Woke up Suna and helped her into the apartment and could still picture Ysrael's eyes, the jut of his chin. He's lived so many lives, I thought as Suna and I entered our bedroom and got ready for bed. So many lives and I can't even figure out this one.

suna

Sometime in the afternoon, after the lunch rush, when Uhmma usually takes her walk down the strip mall for cigarettes and Apa naps in the back office—sometime in the afternoon, when the day seems the hottest, Suna turns on the fan. She stands in front of it and closes her eyes. She can feel the sweat evaporating from her skin. She turns around and feels her hair flying forward against her cheeks, coolness traveling along the back of her neck, her spine. Each shake of her head moves the fan's breeze along her scalp. Suna turns back around and leans into the fan until her lips are inches from the screen surrounding the blade. She leans in and begins to hum.

Mina turns her head from the receipts on the counter and smiles at Suna. The pen drops from Mina's hand as she steps toward the fan. Together, Mina's voice joins Suna's in a chorus of ahhhhs, ohhhs and hmmms.

Soft laughter at the back of the store travels forward until

Ysrael emerges from behind a row of plastic-shrouded clothes. He joins them at the fan, adding his raspy tenor. He leads them along a valley of eeees and zzzzzzs.

Suna hears their voices, their laughter merging together. Their shoulders touching, heads tipped together, each trying not to break the circle even as their faces ache from the effort of keeping back crumbling laughter. She hears them across her oceans until the voices seem to be coming from within her head, her world. She closes her eyes and she holds the moment, holds their voices, their faces, behind her eyelids. Suspended against the darkness. The three of them like that. Just like that.

mina

I pretended to be just passing by. Another trip to the bathroom or to the back office for something I forgot. And even
as I realized how obvious it must be, how ridiculous I must
look, I couldn't help myself. I had to see him. If only for that
nod or that smile. There wasn't much we could say to each
other under Uhmma's watchful gaze. But those moments,
those times that I saw him, made everything bearable. The
heat, the rude customers who double-checked every receipt
finding mistakes where there weren't any, Uhmma looking
over my shoulder to see what I was studying, and even Suna.
Suna, who was always at the edge of my vision. Suna, who
always seemed to be standing behind me, watching. When
Ysrael looked up from the press, his forehead still bunched
with concentration, his eyes searching for mine. When Ysrael
smiled for me, lightness brushed my skin. Made me so giddy,
I had to walk on my tiptoes.

Only Uhmma could bring me back.

Mina-ya, Uhmma said, approaching me at the front counter. She had a men's dark blue suit draped over her arm.

I clinched my jaw in recognition.

Take this, Uhmma said and held it out to me. Jonathon has an important dinner tomorrow night with some people from Stanford.

But it's not closing time. Who will watch the front? I protested.

Uhmma waved me away. Do not worry, Uhmma said. I will do some mending up front until it is time to close. Now hurry. I told Jonathon that you would be there shortly. And do not worry about coming back to the store. We will meet you at home. Make sure to ask Jonathon if he has any more advice for you about college. Make sure you ask all your questions now before he leaves.

I yanked the suit out of Uhmma's hands.

Yah, yah, Uhmma yelled. Be gentle. You will wrinkle it.

Jonathon's black convertible was parked in their driveway. I parked on the street and sat in the car, listening to the last of the song playing on the radio. My hand lingered on the key. I could just leave, I thought. Throw the suit away and pretend I had delivered it. Jonathon had other suits. He would live. I turned off the engine. I just couldn't risk what he might do to make it up to me.

I rang the doorbell and held the suit out in front of me.

The door opened.

"Hey, Mina," Jonathon said. He was dressed for the beach. Long, baggy surfer shorts and a blue T-shirt.

"Here," I said and thrust the suit into his hands. I turned on my heel to leave.

"Wait," he said and stepped forward.

I froze.

"Don't you want to come in?"

"No," I tossed over my shoulder hoping to sound casual. "Uhmma needs me to watch the store."

"Come on, Mina," Jonathon said. "You don't even have time for a cone?"

I sighed. All that time we studied together, we always made time for an ice cream break.

"Come on, Mina. I got your favorite flavor."

I scanned the skies as though looking for rain.

"Look," Jonathon said carefully. "I'm sorry about what I said last time. I just want us to go back to being friends. Can we do that?"

I peeked back over my shoulder to see his face. He smiled.

"Here," he said and stepped back into the house. "I'll leave the door open and you can come in when you're ready. Or you can just leave and that'll be it."

His footsteps receded into the house.

I quickly walked down the path toward my car. Was it going to be that easy? I could walk away and that was it? I stopped. Did he really want us to go back to how it had been before? Would he really let us? I thought of our first study sessions, when all he seemed to do was laugh and imitate my math teacher at the board, spit flying everywhere. I wanted to believe Jonathon. Wanted to believe we could just step away, unharmed, from this car wreck of a friendship that we had created. I turned around.

I stepped into the cool of the house and closed the door behind me. I could hear Jonathon opening and closing the cupboards.

I walked into the kitchen.

"Hi," he said, closing another set of cupboard doors. "I can't find any cones. Would you settle for just a bowl?"

I sat down on a bar stool and nodded. Loud music echoed down the stairs from Jonathon's room. He scooped out the vanilla chocolate fudge ice cream into two bowls. Placed a spoon in each bowl and brought one over to me. He took a seat at the other stool.

I tried to smile at him but the muscles of my face twitched nervously. I bit my lip. Jonathon waved his spoon at me in a salute and dug in. I brought the ice cream up to my lips but couldn't bring myself to taste it. I put down the spoon.

"Not hungry?" Jonathon asked with his mouth full of ice cream.

I shook my head and played with the spoon. I cleared my throat. "What's going on?"

Jonathon waved his spoon at me. "Nothing much. Just a lot of packing. What are you up to?"

I shrugged. "SAT stuff. You know how it is."

Jonathon smiled sympathetically and took another bite of ice cream. "That sucks," he said.

I nodded and watched the edges of my ice cream scoop slowly melt. "I don't know why I'm even bothering to take them."

Jonathon turned to me. "Do you need help? I have some friends who can make it easy on you. It's not that expensive."

I shook my head. "No. No, I don't want any more help. I can't do it that way."

Jonathon rolled his eyes. "What way? Come on, Mina. Don't be naïve. You really think every kid in the room is taking their own tests?"

I didn't respond. Jonathon knew how to make me feel like a goody-goody who had no sense of the world. When he had offered to get me answers for tests or even break into the school's computer, I had refused. It was one thing to lie to Uhmma, but I couldn't face cheating my teachers and the school. I couldn't go that far.

"It's not like those standardized tests are fair or really a measure of intelligence. It's all a way of keeping the classes separated. Upholding the institution of hypocrisy we call academia," Jonathon said.

I played with my spoon and let him rant. Jonathon considered himself a rebel of sorts, trying to undermine the system, cheating the makers of the SAT by taking tests for people who could pay. Jonathon could justify anything. When really he just hated all the expectations his mother heaped on him too. Going to Stanford, becoming a doctor. And while superficially he played the ideal son, underneath, he did everything he could to resist the system. For all of Mrs. Kim's bragging, she wasn't too far from the truth. Jonathon was a computer whiz and a brain. He just didn't like to think of himself that way.

I changed the subject. "You going to Grace's birthday party?" Grace had a beach party every year for her birthday. I hadn't heard from Grace since the last time we had fought at church. She had tried to get me to talk to Jonathon. Make up. I had told her to mind her own business. I missed talking to her.

"Yeah. You want me to pick you up?"

I shook my head.

" 'Cause it's not a problem. How about I pick you up from work after you close. I'm sure your mom will be fine."

"It's okay. I can't go," I lied.

Jonathon snorted and scraped the last spoonful of ice cream from his bowl. "Is it that you can't go, or that you don't want to go? Or maybe you do want to go, but just not with me."

"Stop it, Jonathon." I took a deep breath, tried to keep down the familiar feeling of being overwhelmed and reasoned into doing something.

"Why can't I just hang out with you? You know, we did a lot of that before you got all weird and moody."

I scowled at him. "What are you talking about?" I said.

"I'm just saying that you're acting strange. Even Grace thinks that you've changed."

He was turning all my friends against me. Even Grace. I pushed the ice cream away from me. I stood up to leave. I wasn't going to sit here and let him play games with me. He could do whatever the hell he wanted to do.

Jonathon reached out and grabbed my arm. "Wait, Mina. Don't be like that. Can't we talk without getting into a fight?"

I wrestled my arm away.

"Mina, please stay." He stood up and hugged me to him. "I'm sorry."

I stood in his embrace, my eyes closed, wishing we could really return to being friends again. I felt his lips on my neck.

"Stop it." I tried to step out of his arms.

He tightened his grip around me.

I grabbed one of his fingers, bending it back.

"Damn it." He let go of me. He held on to his finger and yelled, "You know, Mina, every time I try to be nice to you, help you out, you start acting like some freak."

"That's because you always want something in return. I just wanted help," I yelled back.

Jonathon grimaced. "You didn't want help. You wanted me to lie for you. You wanted me to figure out how to forge your report card."

"I didn't ask you to do that." I shook my head. "I didn't ask you," I said weakly.

Jonathon looked away. "And I didn't ask you to fool around with me. You did that on your own."

I reached out, placed a hand on the counter to steady myself. What had begun as two friends talking, then kissing, had spiraled into something else. At first, I didn't mind being with Jonathon. At first, it had been kind of fun. As though we were conspirators in a heist, trying to figure out all the angles and fooling around in between. Only, he started wanting more.

I silently cried, You knew I didn't have a choice. You knew

there was no one else I could have turned to. You knew. I bowed my head and let my tears fall to the floor.

Jonathon turned to me. "I just wanted you to like me. And for a while I thought you did. I thought you really did." He shook his head. "I guess that wasn't it. You were just using me. Right?" He waited a few seconds for me to answer.

When I refused to speak, he yelled, *"Answer me!"*

He strode forward in two steps and grabbed my face, forcing his lips on top of mine until our teeth gnashed together.

I shoved him away and ran for the door. Behind me, Jonathon called out, "Mina, come back. I'm sorry. I was angry. Mina, I just wanted you to give us a chance. Mina, please. Mina."

I slammed the door behind me.

suna

Suna opens her eyes, blinks against the darkness, the shadowless night, and wonders what has woken her, if she has been sleepwalking or if she is in her room. She turns over, and automatically her eyes search for Mina in the other bed.

Mina's huddled form lies sideways, body curled so tight, each vertebra stretches against the thin cotton nightshirt. Suna silently slips out of bed and goes to Mina. Sits at the edge of the bed and places a gentle hand on Mina's shoulder.

Mina cries silently. She bites her knee, her eyes shut tight against the world, and yet the shaking of her body cannot be stopped. Suna does not know the whys. Mina refuses to talk about it. Refuses to talk to anyone. Suna only knows that Mina has been like this before. And like the other times, Suna gently pats her back and says over and over again, Gha-jang, gha-jang.

Suna leans back against the headboard of Mina's bed and closes her eyes. She keeps up her rhythmic soothing song, like a metronome, her lullaby gently urging her sister to quiet and sleep. How many times had Mina done the same for her when she was little and scared from a nightmare. The same refrain muttered over and over again until sleep hooded their eyes. Gha-jang, gha-jang, gha-jang.

mina

Jonathon's words played over and over again in my mind. His angry face flashed in front of me every time I blinked my eyes. Was it my fault? If I hadn't asked him to help me. If I had only told Uhmma the truth. All this would have never happened. Jonathon and I would still be just two friends who had to hang out because we went to the same church and our mothers liked to talk. We would still be watching TV or playing video games.

I kept to myself the whole day, hardly straying from the front register. Ysrael tried to catch my eye a few times, but I ignored him, buried myself in my books. I didn't want to complicate things more than they were already. At the end of the day, I bolted from the store and went home to hide in the closet. I cranked up my CD player and put in my earphones. Time. I needed time to figure this all out. I needed time to come up with another plan. Another way out. I needed a river.

There was a knock at the door.

"What?" I said.

Suna cracked open the door. "Uhn-nee, it's almost time to go to the library."

I sighed. "I don't want to go."

Suna stood up and stated simply, "He'll be waiting."

That was what scared me.

Ysrael was leaning up against his car, one leg kicked back like a flamingo, reading a book when we entered the parking lot. A lock of his straight black hair fell across his forehead. His white T-shirt was worn down so thin, the roundness of his shoulders showed through. Usually he wore a plaid shirt at work. His jeans, slung low on his narrow hips, were splotched white in places where the bleach had splashed.

I drove up next to him and Ysrael looked up from his book with a smile.

"Hey," he said and walked over to our car. Resting his hands on the roof of the car, he peered into Suna's open window. Suna turned in her seat to look at him. They smiled at each other.

I turned away, checking out the usual crowd on the library steps.

Suna spoke softly, boldly. "Hi, Ysrael. Where should we go?"

Ysrael barked a laugh. The kids on the steps looked over at the car. I turned and met Ysrael's inquisitive eyes.

"I don't think it's my decision," Ysrael said.

Suna turned to me. "Uhn-nee?"

"What?" I said.

"Are you going to class?" Ysrael asked.

I sighed and gripped the steering wheel a little tighter. What was I doing? What the hell was I doing? A heaviness spread through my muscles, my limbs. I didn't want to make any more decisions. I didn't want to think anymore.

I shrugged and stared straight ahead. "I don't care." I could feel Ysrael studying me. A car behind us honked. Ysrael looked back and gave a small wave.

Suna spoke up. "Come on. Get in."

Ysrael seemed to be waiting for me. I waved him in. Suna opened her door and flipped her seat forward. Ysrael scrambled into the backseat.

We drove back onto El Cajon Boulevard. The car was silent except for a new steady clicking coming from Sally's engine.

Suna turned in her seat and spoke to Ysrael. "I think Sally has to go in for a checkup."

"The clicking?"

Suna nodded. "It's getting worse."

I snapped, "It is not." I hated when Suna tried to be dramatic. She could make a sad story about anything.

Ysrael leaned forward. "Sometimes a noise is just a noise. And sometimes it just needs a tune-up. And sometimes"—he patted the headrest of the car seat—"you just have to be good to her until the end."

I smiled at Ysrael's words and stopped at a red light. Suna frowned. I glanced back at Ysrael and lifted one shoulder. He tapped Suna on the arm and pointed at a car wash.

"Let's give her a makeover."

Suna's eyes grew wide. "Really? Really? Sally hasn't been washed in a thousand years."

Ysrael bought us purple Popsicles and a car wash for Sally. We sat on the low cement curb that divided up the parking spaces and watched Sally inch forward into the swishing curtains. I licked a cold purple drop before it fell to the ground. Suna kept her eyes on Sally and quickly, methodically, licked her Popsicle without letting one drop fall to the ground.

Ysrael was a biter. Ate his Popsicle in three chomps. Then he chewed on the stick. He watched me lick my Popsicle with a half-curved smile on his face as I tried to take my time, make it last.

Ysrael shook his head at me.

Cool purple drops fell on my knuckles. I licked them off. More purple drops fell at my feet. I switched hands and licked the purple from my fingers. A cascade of purple drops fell to the ground.

"Do I have to take that away from you?" Ysrael asked, the corners of his lips twitching up.

I gave him a menacing look and turned my back to him. Took that Popsicle and ate it up in four quick bites. A cold, sharp headache made me squint in pain. Ysrael leaned forward to see my face. He laughed and laughed. I pushed him on the shoulder. One of his legs shot out and he lost his perch on the cement curb, toppling to the asphalt ground.

Sally sparkled. All her dents and cracks in the paint didn't matter. Her bright, clean whiteness, the clear windshield, the shine off her bumper—she looked brand-new to us. Suna jumped up as soon as Sally was spit out of the car wash and ran to her side. Ysrael and I followed, taking our time, our steps in line.

"Thanks," I said.

Ysrael chewed on his stick. "You didn't look so great when you got to the library."

"Yeah. I just have a lot to think about."

Ysrael raised his eyebrows but didn't press me.

"Can I take you somewhere?" he asked.

"Where?"

"Trust me?" he said.

I took a deep breath. I nodded.

Ysrael directed me along streets I never knew existed. It was a part of El Cajon that climbed high into the desert hills. The city glittered in the horizon. I pulled the car over onto a dirt overlook. Another car in the distance was parked off to the side.

Ysrael stepped out of the car and stretched, hands reaching high for the sky, a smooth brown swatch of his stomach exposed. I stepped out of the car.

"Suna, are you coming?" I asked.

Suna held up a fistful of damp paper towels from the car wash. "In a second. I want to make Sally clean on the inside like on the outside."

Ysrael stepped up on the bumper and sat down on the hood of the car. He leaned back on his hands and threw his head back for a second, before looking forward, taking in the view of the city. The sun had just dropped out of sight, but the sky, streaked with reds and purples and blues, spread out like a canvas lit up from behind. I stepped up onto the bumper and sat down next to Ysrael. High over our heads, the first stars were just beginning to spark.

"I never knew this was here," I said.

Ysrael tipped his head back again and looked up at the stars. "You'd never know that El Cajon was such a pit from up here."

"You hate it here?" I asked.

Ysrael's lips turned down. "Sometimes. Sometimes I can't stand it." He looked at me. "And other times, I can't imagine being anywhere else."

It was my turn to look up at the stars. "I don't know what it's like to be anywhere else."

Ysrael sighed. "There are better places."

I lowered my head and cast my eyes on the city. The lights moved and twinkled in the waves of heat. "Like San Francisco?"

"Yeah," he said.

"You still going?"

"Yeah."

"It sounds like the land of Oz," I said.

Ysrael shrugged. "It did seem like a magical place when I visited. I don't know. Maybe I made it all up. Maybe when I get there, it'll look just like El Cajon."

"Don't say that," I said. "There must have been something about it. Something you saw that made it special."

Ysrael leaned forward and clasped his hands. "I guess."

"Sometimes it's hard to trust that you really do know what's right for you," I said.

Ysrael spoke softly, his eyes on the skyline. "I'm scared. I've been trying to move up to San Francisco for the past year, but I just keep staying around here."

"Where it's comfortable?"

He ran a hand through his hair. "Yeah. Yeah, I guess that's it. It's easier to stay here even if I hate it 'cause it means that I don't have to face what it's like to try something new."

"I think we all do that to some extent or another. I mean, isn't it always easier to stay with what's familiar?" I asked.

"You feel like that?"

I nodded.

Ysrael smiled shyly at me. "I got into music school up there."

I sat up straighter. "That's great!" I beamed. "That is completely perfect. You're gonna be a great musician. I mean, you already play like a pro."

Ysrael shook his head. "I've got a lot to learn. I just don't want to fail. You know what I mean? I want this so badly. I want—" He stopped himself. His hands were balled into fists as though he were ready to fight for his music right now. Right here. He ran the knuckles of his fist along his scar.

He stared out at the skyline. "When it first happened. The accident. All I could do was cry at night. I could be brave as hell all day long, run away from the kids teasing me, act like I didn't care what anyone said. But at night, when everyone went to sleep, that's when I let it all out. My father taught me how to play the guitar then."

Ysrael smiled. "He used to say that I should at least put my wails to music so the neighbors would think that I was singing."

I laughed. Imagined a man, handsome like Ysrael, placing a guitar in his young son's hands.

Ysrael whispered, "I'm afraid I'm just gonna screw it up. Someday, I want to bring my papa here. Bring him across the border so he can point and tell everyone, 'That's my son up there.' " He paused, an embarrassed smile on his face. "You think that's stupid?"

"No," I said. "Not at all. I think it's a beautiful dream."

"Yeah, well, it might never be more than that. A dream."

"Stop being so critical. At least you know what you want to do. At least you have a passion."

Ysrael turned to me. "And you don't?"

I couldn't meet his eyes. I studied my hands. "I've been on a track for so long, I don't know what's beyond it."

"Where is that track supposed to take you?" he asked.

"Harvard."

Ysrael whistled. "You're like one of those Asian geniuses or something."

I grimaced and shook my head. "No. Far from it. It's just what my mom expects, but . . ." I paused, wondering how much I should reveal. Ysrael stayed silent, his dark eyes reflecting the stars.

I whispered, "What if I don't get in? What do I do then?"

"You know, Mina, there are other schools besides Harvard. What's wrong with Berkeley or UCLA?"

"You don't understand," I said. "Those schools aren't the best."

Ysrael shrugged. "Last time I checked, those schools were still pumping out some pretty smart folks."

"Whatever," I said and looked away. "Explain that to my mom."

Ysrael didn't respond. I glanced back at him. He was studying me.

"Maybe you should start by explaining it to yourself first," Ysrael said.

I rolled my eyes, but something about what he said stuck. I could feel it lodged there at the edge of my thoughts.

"You can still change things, Mina," Ysrael said softly. "You can still choose how you're going to live this life."

"Sometimes it's not about choosing. It's about living up to a dream. It's about trying to please the people you love. I don't think there's anything wrong with that. I mean, my mom can be a pain, but she just wants the best for me."

"But what do you want?" Ysrael asked.

I stared at him.

"What do you do that is just for you?" Ysrael asked.

No one had ever asked me that before. I stared up at the sky, afraid to tell him the truth. Compared to how serious Ysrael took his music, what I felt singing at home or in the chorus didn't seem like much. I smiled at Ysrael and shrugged my shoulders.

We were silent as we watched the deep blue of the

night bleed into the sun-soaked sky, leaving behind a trail of stars.

"This is my favorite time of day," Ysrael said. "It's called the gloaming."

I turned the new word over in my mouth. Something fit. "I like it," I said.

Ysrael met my eyes and did not look away. He took a deep breath and kept his eyes on me. We stayed that way. For a second. A minute. A lifetime. Ysrael finally turned back to the sky. He stretched a hand out to the stars, his fingertips reaching for the light.

"Look at those stars. I don't think I've ever seen them this bright. Look," he whispered. "Look at how they shine for you."

I gazed out past his hand. Past the city. Past the blue-black night sky and set my sights on a star.

suna

*I*magine. Two forms. Two separate profiles outlined by the twilight sky and the sparkling lights of a city that lay at their feet. And the stars. The stars. Look how they shine. For them. As though this night, this moment lives suspended in a snow globe filled with glitter.

Suna leans forward between the two front seats and studies these two forms as though they are strangers. He touches her cheek and she leans into his palm, into the hand that cups her face. And he brings that face to his, their foreheads touching, their lips whispering. He strokes her face with the back of his hand, his knuckles tracing the gentle slope of her jaw, her neck. She bows her head, her long hair falling forward. He kisses her forehead, her brow, her temple. She slowly raises her face to his and their lips meet. Gentle as petals falling to the floor.

And so it is. The two forms, the two strangers, in finding

each other, in their union, become recognizable. Mina and Ysrael. Ysrael and Mina.

Suna looks away. She turns her back to them and stares out the rear window, at the craggy, desolate lines of the mountain. Low desert shrubs dot the landscape. She gazes up at the stars, at the deep blue canvas of the night sky, and she feels that emptiness rushing into her body, spreading through her limbs. For stars can only shine against darkness.

mina

I shook the long receipt and tried to concentrate on the numbers again. I had been staring at the same slip of paper for most of the afternoon. It was simple. Refund the amount. Punch in the receipt again, minus a few items, collect the cash that had been "overpaid" and discard the original receipt. Simple. But for some reason, my head kept wandering. Kept listening for Ysrael in the back of the store. I knew I also had to go over yesterday's end of the day totals so that the number of items collected matched the number of items charged so that my refunds weren't so noticeable. Pull it together, I said to myself. I shook my head and pulled the manila envelope out from under the cash register. Uhmma was due back any time now.

I was just redoing some calculations when Ysrael surprised me from behind. He grabbed my hips.

"Ahhh," I yelled and whipped around. "What are you doing?"

Ysrael grinned. "Got you." He kept his hands on my hips, his body close to mine.

I gave him a quick hug and then stepped back, gently peeling back his hands. I glanced out the store window to make sure no one had seen us.

"Hey," I said, suddenly feeling shy.

"Hey, yourself," he said and leaned his back against the counter. "Can I see you tonight?"

I shifted my feet. "I don't know."

Ysrael sighed. "It's not a library night."

"Right."

"Isn't there anything else you have to do?"

"I guess. I have to think about it." Ysrael didn't understand how hard it was to get out of the house. How Uhmma always had a million questions about where I would be, who was going with me. Each lie had to be crafted with care. I busied myself to avoid his gaze. I put the rest of the receipts back in the envelope and placed it under the counter.

"When do you get to do what you want?" he asked quietly, looking away from me.

I reached out, quickly touching Ysrael's hand. "Please, Ysrael—"

Uhmma's voice called from the back, "Mina-ya." Her footsteps were approaching.

I rushed away from Ysrael and tried to meet Uhmma before she saw us together.

Uhmma appeared from behind the clothes and stopped in the middle of the aisle, her eyes squinting at Ysrael, who was still leaning against the front counter.

I stepped into her line of vision. "Hi, Uhmma," I said.

She leaned to one side to see past me. Mina, she said, what is he doing up front?

I raised one hand and gestured as though it was the most natural thing in the world. I had to go to the bathroom and I asked Ysrael to watch the front for one second.

Uhmma frowned. She said, Where is your father and Suna? Are they in the office?

I nodded. Apa is too tired to walk all the way from the back to the front for just one minute. And Suna . . . I let my voice trail away, letting Uhmma come to her own judgment.

She sighed, Hurry up. I will watch the front until you return.

I walked back to the bathroom. I could hear Uhmma's voice growling at Ysrael, "You go back to work. Not for you here."

I hated her.

When I returned from the bathroom, Uhmma was checking over the receipts in the manila envelope. "Okay, Uhmma," I said quickly, hoping she would leave me alone.

Uhmma slid the receipts back into the envelope and placed it under the counter.

Mina, she said, we must get you ready for school.

What do you mean? I asked.

She smiled and said, It is the end of August. Do you not want to get some new clothes? She studied my face. You are acting strangely. Most years, it is you who must remind me to go clothes shopping for the fall.

I nodded. I couldn't believe summer was almost over. For

once, I had absolutely no interest in thinking about what I would be wearing for school. But if I protested, Uhmma would definitely suspect something was wrong.

Uhmma opened the cash register and took out a wad of twenties. She said, Go get your sister. I will meet you at the car after I tell your father.

I scanned the back for Ysrael as I made my way to the rear entrance of the store. He was missing from his usual place at the presses. There was no way to meet him tonight. I would have to explain everything tomorrow night, at the library. If he was there.

Uhmma drove cautiously into the parking lot of the mall. Suna sat in the backseat. She leaned forward suddenly and pointed to a spot in the distance.

"There's one," she called out excitedly.

Uhmma drove up to it. There was a motorcycle parked there. It had been hidden from view by the truck.

Uhmma muttered, I should have known.

Suna was silent.

Uhmma turned to me. Check on your side and I will check on mine. She slowly cruised up and down the aisles, looking for a space.

"Right there, Uhmma," I said, pointing to a woman who was just approaching her car. She held several bags in one hand and a baby in the other. Uhmma stopped the car and turned on her blinker. She sat back in her seat and turned to me.

It has been a while, Uhmma said. I have not had a chance to get you some nice clothes.

I shrugged. "It's okay."

Suna was still silent in back. She never seemed to care that most of her clothes were hand-me-downs. Maybe it would have been different if Suna made a big deal about it like most girls her age. But Suna never seemed to care what she wore or what she looked like. She only worried if her hearing aid showed.

We pulled into the parking space and got out of the car. As we walked toward the entrance of the mall, Uhmma put her hand around my waist, pulling me close. I realized with a start that I had somehow grown taller than Uhmma. It was only by an inch, but for a second, it was as though the world had tipped upside down.

Uhmma directed us when we got inside.

Suna. Uhmma pointed. We will meet you in the children's section.

Suna nodded and headed off slowly in that direction. Suna was still too small to fit into the teen sizes. I thought for a second to go with her, make Uhmma spend time looking at Suna's clothes instead of just rushing through at the last minute, but then the entire process would take longer than I could stand. I followed Uhmma to the teen section.

Uhmma held up a dress. What about this one?

I barely looked up before shaking my head no. Uhmma always liked the fancy things. I rifled through piles of shirts, looking for my size.

Uhmma and I walked over to the dressing rooms with a pile of clothes in both of our arms. I wanted it all to be over. Why was it that I always forgot how painful it was to shop with Uhmma? And then I would be reminded as she battled over what looked good. My head ached from having to fend off all of Uhmma's choices without getting her mad. The saleslady led us to the back and unlocked a door. Uhmma stepped inside with me.

Here, Uhmma said and handed me a dress that I had been too tired to fight off. I kicked off my shoes and took off my T-shirt. Uhmma sat down on the bench with her pile of choices in her lap. I pulled the dress over my head. The reflection in the mirror was as awful as the dress felt against my skin. The pale green color made me look as though I should have been working at a hospital except that the dress had tiny, fake pearl buttons down the middle. More like a nurse at a nursing home. I reached down to pull off the dress.

Mina, Uhmma said, you did not even take off your jeans. How can you tell if it looks good if it is bunched at your jeans?

"I don't like it," I said and rushed to pull it off.

Uhmma stopped my hand. She said, Take off your jeans and let us look to see how it really fits.

I made a small grunt but sometimes it's just easier to do what Uhmma wants. I stepped out of my jeans and looked in the mirror.

Uhmma smoothed the skirt. There, she said. That looks nice. Maybe you could wear that for graduation. Uhmma smiled up at me. She shook her head. You have become a young lady. Aigoo, Mina, your uhmma is getting old.

Uhmma's eyes softened around the edges. She spoke in a whisper, If only Harvard were not so far away. Maybe Stanford would be a better choice. Aii, but Harvard is the best. I do not believe what Mrs. Kim says. Harvard will always be more respectable than Stanford.

"Stop, Uhmma," I said, reaching down to pull the dress off.

What, Uhmma said. I am only saying what is true. You have worked so hard. I could not be more proud of you, Mina-ya. What is wrong with that?

I struggled out of the dress and handed it back to her. I reached over to my chosen pile of clothes and picked up some new jeans and a blue shirt. I didn't answer her.

With my new clothes, including the ugly green dress, folded into neat square piles inside my shopping bag, we walked toward the children's section. Uhmma started scanning the racks. I went to find Suna.

I found her in one of the dressing rooms. She sat in her underwear and training bra, clutching a dress to her chest. Her body was still so young, without any hints of change. Suna held out the dress. It was a grown-up sort of dress made of a silky material with thin straps and a short skirt, not the kind that was usually hanging up in the children's section. It was a dress that one of the girls sitting on the front steps of the library would have worn. It was a dress for teenagers.

"Do you think Uhmma will let me have it?" she asked.

I knew what Uhmma would think. But Suna's face, so wide and open with hope, would not let me answer any other way. "Yes," I said. "I'll talk to her."

As I was stepping out of the dressing room, I asked, "When did you start wearing the bra?"

Suna smiled. "A long time ago. You've been too busy to notice."

I smiled back and left with the dress in my hands.

Uhmma refused. She had a few T-shirts and jeans picked out. I held out the dress again.

She only wants this, I insisted.

That is too old for her, Uhmma argued. She does not need to wear those kinds of clothes.

What is wrong with it? This is what the other teenagers her age are wearing.

Uhmma snapped, She is not like the other girls.

But she is, Uhmma, I pleaded. She could be just like them. Her hearing aid does not make her . . .

I struggled to find the right Korean word for it and couldn't. I switched to English. "She's not some kind of freak."

Uhmma ignored me and walked toward the cash register to pay for the clothes. I stood in my place. I couldn't believe Uhmma would not let Suna have one dress. The one thing she wanted. We had been living and acting the way Uhmma wanted us to for all our lives. Doing anything to uphold appearances. When did we get to choose what we wanted?

I walked after Uhmma. When are you going to stop making Suna pay for your mistakes? I asked.

Uhmma stopped walking. She wouldn't look at me, just stated simply, Stop it, Mina.

No, you stop, Uhmma. Suna is as much your daughter as I am.

I never said that she was not my daughter, Uhmma said angrily.

No, I said. You just act like it.

Uhmma stepped back, her eyes squinted in anger and pain. Why are you saying all this? she said. Why are you acting like this?

I stepped forward with the dress. I held it out to her and said, She needs you, Uhmma. She needs you to show that you love her too.

Uhmma sighed. Suna stepped out of the dressing room area and walked toward us, her smile wide with hope. I studied Uhmma's face. And though I couldn't see it, I sensed something, like blue skies waiting behind the fog. Uhmma finally took the dress from my hands.

On our way out, Uhmma stopped to touch a red silk jacket on a mannequin. She held the sleeve for a moment and then let go.

That would look good on you, I suggested. The tingling guilt of watching Uhmma count out all her twenties at the register softened my tone with Uhmma.

Uhmma shook her head. She said, I am too old to be wearing such a bold color. The fabric is nice, though.

Do you want to check and see if they have other colors? You could go and try it on, I urged.

Uhmma shook her head again. Maybe another time, she said. We are done for today.

We walked out of the store, the faint classical music fading into the background. The weight of the shopping bag cut into my wrists.

suna

She lets the silky material slide over her head. The thin straps fall against her collarbone, the short skirt brushing the tops of her knees. Suna stares at herself in the mirror. The reflection that gazes back at her does not seem like her own. The girl in the mirror seems far older.

Suna twirls around and checks again. Same reflection. Suna smiles and finds the girl smiling back. Suna kicks out one long leg. The reflection does the same. Suna adjusts the straps. Smoothes the fabric against her flat stomach. This dress will make all the difference. This dress will show everyone that she is not just a little girl anymore. Suna gazes into her eyes. She wants Ysrael to see her this way. She wants Ysrael to see that she can be beautiful too.

mina

*H*e ignored me the entire day. Not even looking up when I walked over to the press to hang up some white dress shirts on a stand next to him. I tried to catch his eyes, but he refused to look up. Did he really think that I didn't want to see him yesterday? Was he angry that I hadn't stood up for him?

So what was I expecting when I drove into the library parking lot, scanning all the cars, and found no trace. There was no familiar figure leaning up against the door. No familiar profile bowed in concentration. Suna sat next to me, craning her neck, her eyes searching. I parked the car and tried to act as though I had really come to the library to go to the prep class. I twisted in my seat and reached for my books on the backseat. As I stretched out, a sharp pain in my shoulder made me cry out.

"Goddamnit." I slumped in my seat, the heel of my hands pressing into my eyes. Suna sat quietly next to me. I counted my breaths, willing the tears to recede, willing my heart to stop beating. Like that. Like I cared. What did I expect when I couldn't even be honest with myself about my feelings?

Even before I heard his voice, I knew Ysrael had come by the small yelp of joy from Suna. I took my hands from my face and looked up.

"Mina," he said, his head tilted in concern. "Are you okay?"

I nodded.

"You sure?"

"Hi, Ysrael," Suna called out and smoothed her new dress across her lap.

Ysrael smiled at her. "Hey, Suna. Can you wait here for a minute while I talk to your sister?" Ysrael opened the car door for me. I stepped out.

"Are you going somewhere?" Suna asked, leaning forward.

"We're just gonna talk over there." Ysrael pointed to some trees at the edge of the parking lot. "Okay?" Ysrael leaned into the car and tousled Suna's hair.

We walked over to the trees. Halfway across, he took my hand.

"What's going on?" Ysrael asked, giving my hand a squeeze.

I thought about what to say. If I should tell him the truth or just lie about how Uhmma had been giving me a hard time. I thought about all the lies in my life. All the lies that had become my life, and I knew in that moment Ysrael would not be a part of that. I wouldn't lie to him.

"I thought you weren't going to be here," I said.

Ysrael took my other hand. "Where would I be?" he asked.

I shook my head, not trusting my voice.

He reached out and touched my face. "Mina. I don't know how to be with you. One minute you're acting like you can't wait to hang out with me. And the next minute, as soon as your mom walks in, you act like I'm nobody. I don't know how to deal with that."

I struggled to get my voice back. "My mother makes it hard. I have to do things that I don't want to because of her."

His voice was worn down. "Come on, Mina. This isn't about your mom or what you can or can't do. You're not a child. You do have a mind of your own."

"You don't understand," I said. "I can't just do whatever I want all the time like you. There are people I have to take care of."

Ysrael clasped his fingers behind his neck. He gazed off at the traffic. "I know you have to watch out for Suna. I understand. But, Mina." He turned to me. "You can't protect her forever. And you can't live to please your mother all the time. When are you going to stop hiding and live your own life?"

I stared down at my hands. At the lines in my palm. So many paths. And at each intersection, a choice. A decision. In all those lines, where was my lifeline?

Ysrael offered me his hand. I reached out and took it.

"Come on," he said. "Let's go and get something to eat."

Ysrael sat in the backseat, his guitar to one side. Every once in a while, he would lean forward to direct me.

"Take a right at that next corner."

I turned.

"There it is," he said, pointing.

A red neon sign in cursive read Juan's. A curly wrought-iron fence alongside the short flight of stairs to the front door was the only decoration. The small windows were dark with drawn curtains. If the sign wasn't out front, you would have thought it was just another apartment in a run-down building. I parked the car alongside the street.

"You sure it's open?" I asked, opening the car door and stepping out. I pushed my seat forward to let Ysrael out.

"Don't worry, you'll see," Ysrael said and scrambled out with his guitar.

Ysrael led us up the steps and then opened the door to the restaurant. An entire world roared back at us.

Tables were packed with families, with men, with teenagers. Waiters and waitresses rushed back and forth from a small swinging door in the back of the restaurant. We stood at the cash register and waited for someone to seat us. A young waitress in the back with long reddish brown hair scowled at us. There were no empty tables as far as I could see, but Ysrael waved at a heavyset waiter with a short, graying mustache and dark, slicked-back hair. The man nodded at Ysrael, holding up one finger. He took the paper menus from the people at the table and came forward to us.

"Hola, Ysrael," the man said and gave Ysrael a quick thump on the chest with his forearm.

"Cómo estás, Miguel," Ysrael said.

Miguel waved his fingers in the air. "Busy, busy. Who you got with you?"

"These are my friends," Ysrael said. "Mina, Suna, this is Miguel. He manages the restaurant."

"Hi," I said and reached out to shake his hand.

Suna stood slightly behind me, peeking out, and waved a quick hello.

"Okay if we sit in the back?" Ysrael said and pointed his chin toward a dark room off to the side.

Miguel smiled and nodded. "No problem. I'll bring some food back there."

Ysrael nodded and then raised one eyebrow. "How about a couple of tacos?" He stopped and turned to us. "Do you eat pork?"

I nodded.

Ysrael turned to Miguel. "And some carnitas with rice and beans."

Miguel didn't bother to write it down but simply tapped his order pad against his hand.

"Sí, sí. Ysrael, you might have to work with that jukebox. It gave us some problems last night."

Ysrael gave him a thumbs-up before gently taking my hand and leading me through a narrow path between the tables. I turned around and caught Suna's hand and pulled her along.

Ysrael turned on the lights and the red tablecloths glared out at us. The room was about the size of our bedroom and painted turquoise. Small round tables lined the perimeter and an old jukebox stood at one end. He walked over to the jukebox and laid his guitar along the top before he bent down to remove the front panel. Suna stood against the wall and stared around the room, her eyes taking in all the posters lining the walls. Beer advertisements with dark-haired, sexy, pouting women hung next to pictures of ancient ruins and photos of beautiful blue-green oceans and white-sand beaches.

I sat down at one of the small tables and waved Suna over. She didn't see me; her eyes flickered from poster to poster. I stood up and walked over to her.

"Suna," I said in a loud whisper near her ear.

"Hmm," she said.

"Come sit down. You look like a dork standing there."

She pried her eyes away from one particular poster with a beautiful beach sunset. We took seats at a table close to Ysrael.

It was the smell before the voice that made us turn around.

"Here you go," Miguel said and set the steaming plates on the table.

The tacos sat in a row, overflowing with diced tomatoes and shredded lettuce. On a separate plate was the rice and softly mounded beans covered with a sprinkling of cheese. There was also a platter of shredded meat sitting in thin brown gravy, which I had never seen before. Miguel placed a basket with a lid on the table.

Suna opened the basket. "Tortillas," she said.

As Miguel left, he placed a hand on Ysrael's shoulders and turned him to our table. Ysrael stood up and wiped his hands on his jeans.

It did not take us long to sample everything on the platters. Ysrael showed us how to eat the carnitas and we didn't need any explanation for the tacos. Ysrael propped his elbows on the edge of the table and rested his chin in his hands. He watched me eat. I was just putting the tortilla wrapped up with carnitas and some rice and beans into my mouth.

"You can eat," he said.

I grinned at him and then kept on chewing. It was all so good. I had eaten Mexican food before, but the carnitas were something else. I licked the juice from the corner of my lips. Ysrael laughed and touched my cheek before standing up. He walked over to the jukebox and punched a few buttons.

Ysrael picked up his guitar and placed the strap over his head. Pulling a chair over, he rested one foot on the seat and began to fiddle with the strings of his guitar. The sound of an old record, scratchy with age, radiated from speakers high above us in the corners of the room. Soon, quick guitar playing and a woman's voice singing in Spanish filled the air. A few people wandered over to the doorway of the small room. I finished my tortillas and took a sip of the watermelon agua fresca that Miguel had brought over after we had started eating.

Ysrael had his eyes closed, his head nodding in time to the music, his fingers tapping out a beat on the body of his guitar. More people gathered at the doorway and then began to spill into the room. Ysrael opened his eyes and searched for me. He smiled when he caught my eyes. He held me in his gaze and the music began.

This was nothing like the beach. This was fast and furious with an edge of playfulness that wove in and out of the song, sometimes in harmony, sometimes on an entirely different path. But somehow, whatever Ysrael played, it made sense. More people entered the room, sitting down at the tables, lining the walls. Suddenly, the formerly empty room was so crowded, I could hardly see past the bodies to where Ysrael still stood, one leg on the chair, guitar nestled against his body. The first song ended and another began, this one even faster. The same woman was singing on the jukebox, but this time when her voice held a note, Ysrael's tenor joined her. A few people yelled their encouragement. Ysrael sang loudly, evenly. His eyes closed, his head swaying with a grace that could only come from being inside the music. He sang as though he belonged.

I felt a tapping on my shoulder. Suna's eyes opened wide, her hands gesturing madly with excitement. She pointed at Ysrael and mouthed something I couldn't make out. I shook my head to show her that I couldn't hear. She nodded and went back to listening. Her head bobbed along to the music. The people standing were swaying and dancing. I stared around the room, amazed at the way Ysrael could hold an audience this big. His body rocked to the beat of the song and his hands flew over the guitar strings. I closed my eyes and focused on his voice. And though I didn't understand the words, I still sat with his voice spread out before me like a blanket fluttering in the wind. The music ended and the crowd clapped loudly. I opened my eyes.

Ysrael was laughing, his arm around a waitress's waist. It was the girl who had been scowling at us when we first entered the restaurant. Her long reddish hair framed her face, making her pale skin glow like moonlight. The dusty pink of her lips set off by her dark wide-set eyes. She leaned down and nuzzled Ysrael's neck before she stepped back to let him play the next song. As she receded into the crowd, she looked over in my direction. There was no scowl this time, just a simple direct look. A gaze that held all the confidence of someone who belonged exactly right where she had been standing.

suna

*S*una feels the thumping of people's feet, the vibration of Ysrael's playing and the music from the jukebox. Waves of sound pass over and through her like a breeze. She stands, unable to contain herself, and joins the crowd. And for one of the few times in her life, she experiences the sensation of being a part of something. Amongst these strangers who would not know her from someone on the street, she finds herself clapping and bumping into shoulders and sharing smiles.

Suna tries to memorize every bit of the moment. As if she is filling a box with collected treasures. The feel of her dress against her skin as she moves her body to the music. The blazing smile that Ysrael shines out at her over everyone's head. The pulsing music that fills her head until she begins to feel like she's flying. She wonders briefly if this is why Mina always listens to music. Because it can take you to another place. And even when it seems that the box could not possibly fit another second, Suna pushes in another memory. She grabs on to that poster of the sunset. Of the sun, brilliant and bright, shining out over turquoise waters. She finds it hard to imagine that this is the same sun she sees every day. And as she closes up her box, she promises herself, someday, she will find that place. Walk along those shores and greet the sun like a long-lost friend. Now she knows that this sun can exist.

mina

*H*e didn't even know I left. I stepped out of the restaurant into the hot, windless night and sat on the steps. The music thumped behind the closed door and I rested my forehead against the wrought-iron fence. The face of the waitress and the way she pressed herself against Ysrael lingered on. Of course, I said to myself, of course. Why wouldn't he have someone? I pressed my forehead more deeply into the iron. How stupid I felt. All this time I only saw him as someone whose life bordered with mine. His life at the dry cleaners, his life at the library. But that was my life, not his. He had far more than that. I wiped away the tears with the heel of my palm. And I was not a part of this. His life.

I stood up. I couldn't even be angry with him, at the way he made me feel as though we could be together, at the kiss. Just a sadness so deep, it hurt to move. I took one step at a time and walked away from the restaurant. Walked away from

Ysrael. I didn't know where I was going, just knew that I had to get away from there.

The farther I got, the easier it was to walk until I found myself running. Running hard, block after block, my breath coming in quick pants and sweat running down my back. A large dog leaped against a fence, barking wildly, and I jumped from the sidewalk to the street. The darkness of the street swirled in. The dog snarled and barked again. I crossed to the other side and looked up and down the empty street.

A dart of panic. What was I doing? Where was I going? I wrapped my arms around me and started walking back to the restaurant.

I walked quickly, not looking up, keeping the strangeness of the street and the fear of being alone at the edge of my vision.

In the distance a voice shouted, "Hey."

I looked up. Ysrael was waving and running toward me.

"Mina," Ysrael said in between breaths. "What happened?"

I shrugged.

"Hey," Ysrael said, touching my shoulder. "What's going on?"

I jerked off his hand. "I'm fine."

Ysrael tried to make a joke. "My playing that bad?"

I didn't answer. I turned to walk away.

"Mina." Ysrael grabbed me from behind and hugged me tight, making me stop. "Mina, talk to me."

Ysrael gently turned me around and pulled me against him. "Mina. Mina," he repeated over and over again.

I bowed my head and leaned into him. Let his chest take the brunt of my crying. I could smell the smoky sweetness of his sweat. Felt the hot flush of his skin beneath his thin T-shirt. I shook my head and muttered, "I don't know what I'm doing. I don't belong with you."

Ysrael held me tighter. "Don't say that."

I looked up at him. His face was in shadow, a distant streetlight barely illuminating the slope of his nose and the curve of his lips.

"You live in such a different world."

I could see the shadow of a slight smile. "No, Mina. We make our own world and the restaurant, that place, that's where I go to give back. To make people happy." He laughed. "It's just the only place that'll let me is all."

"But they're your community. They know you." I thought of the waitress and the way everyone shouted out their encouragement. "And they love you."

Ysrael sighed. "Yeah, that's where I'm most comfortable, I guess. But that doesn't mean that's where I'll always be. It's like your family. You know that they'll always be there for you, but you can't base your whole life on them."

I stepped back from Ysrael. "It's easy for you to talk like that, you have someplace to go. You have something that's yours. You have your music." I raised up my hand as Ysrael tried to talk and step toward me. "And you have your girl-friend."

He looked away from me. I knew it. I had made him pause. She was a part of his life. I closed my eyes. And who was I? To him.

He spoke softly, without looking at me. "Helena was my girlfriend. But she isn't anymore. She's someone I care about, but she's not with me."

"It looked like she was with you," I said.

Ysrael nodded. "I understand."

"Is that all you have to say?" I said angrily. Who was he to lead me on? What did he think he was doing?

Ysrael shoved his hands into his pockets, his eyes cast down. "Look, Mina. Helena and I have been broken up for a long time. It has nothing to do with you and me."

I rolled my eyes.

"Mina." Ysrael reached out and touched my elbow, trying to get me to look at him.

I refused to meet his eyes and started to walk back down the street to the restaurant.

Ysrael caught up to me and walked beside me.

"Mina, please just listen. Helena was my first love. We have this history together. I can't explain it, but I will always be there for her, but that doesn't mean we're together. We're just friends."

I remembered her gaze, her confidence. "Yeah, well, maybe she doesn't see it that way."

Ysrael sighed. "I can't answer that for her. All I know is that I don't want to be with her. I don't look at her and want to memorize every little thing she does. I don't think about ways to write songs for her. Or how I can get her to smile. Or worry that she's not looking out for herself enough." He took a deep breath. "I do that with you."

I stopped walking and lifted my eyes up to the stars as

though I could find an answer. As if I could chart a path, navigate my way out of all this confusion.

"Sometimes I feel so lost," I told Ysrael. "I don't know what I'm doing. I've been living with all these lies for so long. I can't tell what's real anymore."

"What do you mean?"

"I don't have the grades for Harvard," I said. "All lies to keep my mother happy." I paused. "And I stole money so I could disappear next fall. Just go somewhere and pretend that I was at Harvard."

I kept my eyes on a star. "Only . . . now there's you. And I don't want you to be a lie. I don't want you to be something I just made up. I want us to be real."

I could feel his gaze holding my face.

I took a deep breath and met his eyes. "Remember how you asked me once what I did for me?"

Ysrael nodded.

"I listen to music. And sing. Sometimes in a chorus, but most of the time at home."

Ysrael smiled.

"It's the only thing that keeps me from going crazy. It's the only thing that feels like mine. When I watch you playing, that look you get, I know that feeling. Even though I can't play guitar or make music." I stared down at my empty hands and whispered, "When I listen to you play, I know how the whole world just falls back when you close your eyes. That longing to be inside the music. To feel yourself soar."

Ysrael reached out for me. I didn't step back. He took another step. The streetlight was closer now. A swatch of his thick black hair fell against his forehead, across his eyebrow. The soft brown crest of his nose. The shadowed moon of his scar. The shy brown of his eyes. So clear. Like stars.

His face tipped toward mine. His lips, the delicate bow of his lips, reached for mine. His hands slipped through my hair, behind my neck, cradling me against him. I closed my eyes and let myself fall forward. This was my world. I stood up on my tiptoes and ran my hands through his hair. Touched my cheek to his cheek. Glanced my lips across his forehead. This was my world. I pressed my lips to his and tasted the sweet gentleness of his tongue. A weakness stilled my heart. He was my world.

suna

A girl. A ghost. Lost. In her own home. She walks in her sleep, a worn stuffed dog hanging from one hand, weaving, bumping between the couch, the chair, the coffee table. Her thin frame slants left as though a stick figure leaning into the wind. And her face. Her face. A landscape of moods. Emotions dancing across still waters. A smile, a grimace, a grin, eyes twitching beneath closed lids, forehead bunching, then smooth, placid. Peaceful.

Outside, thunderclouds gather, pushing a stormy wind through the open windows, rustling the large white T-shirt she wears for pajamas, but her sweat-dampened hair clings to her skin like ivy. She stands still for a moment, even in her sleep, to relish the breeze cooling the sweat on her face. She walks past the bookcase, stumbles against the low television stand, but catches herself before falling. Though she has lived in this apartment her whole life, she walks with the hesitant, slow gait of an intruding stranger.

Her shin bumps against the couch and without reason, without a sigh, her nighttime ambling comes to an end. And like all the other nights, her restless body eases onto the couch cushions, her mind sinks back into a deeper sleep. The stuffed dog is clutched to her side, her cheek presses against the rough grain of the armrest. The pool of her face stills. Calms. Sleeps. The rain begins to fall.

mina

The rain tapping gently on the window above my bed woke me. I kept my eyes closed and listened to the soothing rhythm. Each beat, each note was as whole and singular as the feel of Ysrael's lips on mine. And my heart, once more, fell through space, as though streaking through the night sky.

I cautiously opened my eyes, but Suna's bed was empty. My body stretched out in pleasure at being alone with my thoughts. I turned onto my back and gazed out the window. Wondered what Ysrael was doing. If he was at the dry cleaners yet. I pictured the deep brown of his eyes, that slow smile spreading across his face every morning as I entered the store. I missed him so much.

I dressed quickly and went to wake up Suna. She was still asleep in the living room. I jostled her awake and then sped to the bathroom. When I returned, Suna was still on the couch, sitting up, but definitely not ready to go.

"Come on," I urged, impatient to get to the dry cleaners.

"Leave me alone," she said, her voice edged with anger.

I looked at her in surprise. "Somebody got up on the wrong side of the bed."

"Shut up," Suna said and stood up. She walked to our bedroom.

I followed after her. "What's going on, Suna?" I asked, slightly amused at her defiance. Maybe she was turning into a real teenager after all.

Suna walked into the room and turned around, closing the bedroom door on my face.

"Suna, what's wrong?" I called through the closed door.

"You just left me," her muffled but angry voice replied.

"What?"

"You and Ysrael just left me at the restaurant by myself with all those strangers. You didn't even think about how I would feel."

I sighed. She was right. Last night, as we drove home, she had been strangely quiet, but I had not paid any attention, so lost in my own thoughts.

"I'm sorry," I said loudly, but got no response.

We drove to the dry cleaners in silence. Suna kept her face turned toward the window and wouldn't respond to anything I said. I finally gave up trying to apologize.

Suna and I walked into the dry cleaners and Uhmma's shrieks hit us at the door.

"GET OUT!" Uhmma screamed.

Suna and I ran to the front of the store. Uhmma and Ysrael were squared off in front of the cash register. Apa stood off to the side by the fan. Suna and I stopped in our tracks. My heart began to quicken in realization and dread.

"YOU THIEF!" Uhmma spat out, her eyes narrowed, a look of disgust creasing her forehead.

Uhmma picked up the phone. "I call the police. You leave or I call right now."

Ysrael slowly shook his head and turned to me.

The room began to pulse. The smells of all the chemicals sharp in my nose. My mouth watered in anticipation of the nausea. I had to tell Uhmma. I had to clear Ysrael. But the words, sharp as a fish bone, stayed lodged in my throat. Ysrael stared at me, waiting for me to tell the truth. I lowered my eyes.

Ysrael stepped back, turned around and walked out the front door. We all stood in our places, watching his proud straight back crossing the parking lot and finally disappearing along El Cajon Boulevard.

Uhmma was the first to move. She sat down at the sewing table and began hemming a dress as though nothing had happened. Apa and Suna both faded back into the curtain of clothes.

Uhmma carefully placed a pin in the fabric of the dress.

Still trembling from the encounter, I slowly walked to the register. Tried to keep my voice steady. Calm. "How do you know Ysrael was stealing from us?"

Uhmma raised the hem to her squinting eyes and re-placed the pin. She said, I checked the receipts and they do not match with the money or the clothes we have been cleaning. I knew this would happen. I knew it. He is lucky we did not call the police.

I pressed my lips together. It took every ounce of concentration to keep from running out the door and looking for Ysrael. I told myself, don't make it worse.

Maybe the books were wrong, I said.

Uhmma frowned and said, Do not be ridiculous. I checked the books myself. And when I asked him, he did not even protest.

Uhmma mumbled to herself as she worked, I do not know what we are going to do without Apa being able to work. How can we afford more help? Aigoo. This life will not give us any breaks. Uhmma continued sewing, her shoulders hunched forward with the weight of her worries.

I walked away from her, unable to speak. Unable to burden her further with the knowledge that it was her own daughter causing all this grief. What good would it have done? And yet, what about Ysrael? What about his name? I went to the back office and shut the door. Hid my face in my hands like a coward.

I stayed quiet the entire day. Each time the phone rang, I picked it up with the hope of hearing Ysrael's voice. I held on to that hope until the late afternoon when the phone rang and I picked it up to hear a familiar voice.

"Hi, Mina."

I wanted to hang up.

"Mina?" Jonathon said. "Mina, you there?"

"What is it, Jonathon?" I asked.

"I'm leaving tomorrow."

"Oh," I replied.

"I want to see you today. Tell your mom I found some more books."

I stayed silent.

"Come by my house after you close up."

I ran my hand slowly along the edge of the register, pressing my skin against the sharp metal edge. "I can't," I lied. "I have a prep session at the library."

"No, you don't," Jonathon said. "I have the disk for the report cards. I'll be waiting for you." He hung up.

Uhmma nodded readily when I asked for permission to pick up more books from Jonathon. As I was leaving, Suna followed after me.

"I'm coming with you," she said. "I know you're going to look for Ysrael."

"No, I'm not. I have to pick up some books from Jonathon," I said and picked up my car keys.

"But then, you're going to look for Ysrael," she said stubbornly.

I couldn't lie to her. I nodded.

We left together for Jonathon's house and by the time we got there, I was grateful Suna was with me.

As we walked up Jonathon's driveway, I reached down and squeezed her hand for comfort.

"Are you okay?" Suna whispered.

I turned to her, relieved that she was not still angry. Her forehead was creased with worry. I ran my hand along the smooth length of her hair and forced a smile on my face to reassure her.

When Jonathon opened the door, his eyes shifted between Suna and me. Finally, he held the door open wider. "Come on in."

We stepped into the silent house. Jonathon pointed to the den off the kitchen.

"You can watch TV, Suna," Jonathon said loudly.

"She can hear you," I hissed at him.

Jonathon waved me off. "Your sister and I are going to be busy, so don't just come wandering upstairs. We want privacy. Okay?" he said, his voice still cranked up.

Suna shrank back from Jonathon.

I held up my hand and mouthed, "Five minutes."

Suna nodded.

I let go of her hand and walked upstairs.

Jonathon waited until I stepped inside and then rushed to close the door.

"Why did you have to bring your sister?" he asked angrily.

I shrugged. "She has to go to the library afterward," I said.

"Yeah, right," Jonathon snorted. "You don't trust me? You think I'm gonna try something on you?"

I stepped over to his window, pretending I hadn't heard him.

Jonathon walked over to his desk and picked up a CD.

"You want this?"

I stared at it for a moment. At what was being offered. And for once I didn't care. All that had happened this morning, my betrayal of Ysrael, made every lie stand out for what it was. I studied the lines on my palm. I could choose another path.

Jonathon walked over to me.

"Take it," he insisted with a look on his face, no different than when we were ten and fighting about who got to control the remote while our mothers gossiped in the kitchen. That same damn scrunched-up face. I reached out for him. Stepped toward him.

"Johnny. Please."

His entire body sagged. The slope of his shoulders, the defiant jut of his chin, the anger in his eyes.

"Johnny. I never meant for everything to get so out of control. I didn't know what to do. It just seemed so much easier to lie to my mom, to myself, to you, than face the truth. You know what I mean?" I asked him. He still wouldn't look at me.

"You're the only other person who knows how it is. The way they expect us to bring them the world. How much they need us to be perfect. Johnny, I know you understand. I just couldn't disappoint her."

Jonathon leaned his forearm on top of the window sash and rested his chin on the back of his hand. His voice was low and edged with tiredness. "What did you think you were doing, Mina? Why would you lead me on unless it was to use me. Explain that to me, Mina."

Jonathon turned and faced me.

I breathed out slowly. I wanted to be honest with Jonathon. For once.

"I don't know if I can even explain it to myself," I said, my eyes steady on his. "I guess I wanted to like you. I wish I could have been what you wanted. But everything I had worked for was turning into a lie. Everything I was supposed to be." I paused, trying to find the right words. "The only thing that I could hold on to was you. I wanted something to make sense. If we could be together, then I wasn't just getting you to lie for me. It was like we were doing it for the thrill. To see what we could get away with. Like it was a game."

Jonathon scowled. "It was never just a game with me," he said.

"I tried to end it," I said, fighting back. "But every time I tried to talk about it, you kept telling me that we could go slow. But then we never did. And that time, that last night . . ." I bowed my head so he couldn't see the embarrassment coloring my face.

"But you didn't say anything, Mina. You didn't say no," Jonathon stated.

"I don't know." I shook my head. "I don't know. I was too scared to say anything. It happened so fast."

"Jesus, Mina. We were on the bed. What did you think would happen?" Jonathon asked angrily.

I remembered the pain. The way I had dug my nails into my skin to keep myself from crying out, before I pushed him off me. Before it went any further. And how confused and horrible I felt as I grabbed my clothes off the floor and ran to the bathroom. Jonathon following after me. Knocking on the bathroom door, asking me if everything was all right.

I whispered, "It was my first. Time."

Jonathon stepped away from me, his eyes still cast down. "Yeah, well. It was for me too."

We were silent, the words we had spoken spiraling through the air like bits of dust caught in sunlight. The truth of Jonathon's words spread out before me. All that bragging. All that posturing about how many girls he had dated.

Jonathon's voice cracked as he spoke. "I just wanted a chance, Mina. I just wanted you to give us a chance. I thought I could convince you."

I looked away, out the window, over the houses.

"There was this part of me that couldn't quite believe you liked me. I mean, why all of a sudden would you want to go out with me? All that time I liked you and you never even called my house unless your mom made you. I guess I wanted proof. I wanted something real." Jonathon bowed his head. "I'm so sorry, Mina. I didn't mean to hurt you. I wanted you to like me. The way—" Jonathon stopped. He turned back to the window and gazed out. He exhaled slowly, as though pushing out the memory along with the pain.

"The way I loved you."

I nodded, afraid to speak, afraid my voice would crack. All the years that we had known each other. All those years of growing up together. I wished I could follow the path back, retrace our footsteps. Find the history of us hidden in a room, waiting to be released.

"I'm sorry," I whispered.

I left him standing there, the disk still in his hand. Alone by the window. I stepped away from all the hurt, all that had gone so painfully wrong. I walked forward.

suna

*T*he voices of Mina and Jonathon arguing float down the stairs. Suna tiptoes from the den into the marble foyer. She strains to hear the conversation, but her hearing aid hisses for a moment, the fuzzy static interfering. Suna adjusts the plastic piece, but the reception does not change. Suna sighs and sits on the bottom step. She knows there is something going on with Mina and Jonathon. She wonders how Mina and Jonathon fit together. Certainly not the way Mina and Ysrael fit together. Suna has seen the longing in Jonathon's face every time he speaks to Mina. Has seen the way Mina ignores him. That is until recently. Does Mina love Jonathon? Suna moves that piece into place and studies the picture. No. Suna quickly takes that thought away. Mina could never love someone like Jonathon. Someone so different from Ysrael.

Suna frowns. She refuses to believe what she has heard from Uhmma. Refuses to believe that Ysrael could do anything to hurt them. And yet, what did happen? Why has Mina been so secretive lately? What is Mina planning? Where is the money? Suna sighs and takes out her hearing aid. She rests her chin in the palm of her hand. Sometimes she wishes she had a manual that explains why people act the way they do. The chapter on love would be a million pages long. A million pages plus one page at the very end. Like a "p.s." at the end of a letter.

Love is unexplainable.

mina

*T*he rain fell in abrupt bursts, increasing with the wind, dying down to almost nothing a minute later. Suna and I drove slowly through the library parking lot, our eyes scanning the cars.

I couldn't find the beat-up Ford anywhere.

I headed down the side lot. My breath escaped in a small cry. Ysrael stood under the small overhang at the side entrance, writing in a notebook.

"Suna," I said without looking at her. "Suna, you have to wait in the library."

"What?"

"You have to stay at the library. Ysrael and I have to talk about what happened."

"Why can't I go with you?"

" 'Cause you can't."

"Please, Uhn-nee. I don't want to wait by myself."

"Suna, just do this for me. Please."

Her eyes filled with tears. "Uhn-nee, I want to go with you and Ysrael. You used to take me everywhere. Did I do something? Why are you always trying to leave me behind now?"

My voice softened. "No, Suna, you didn't do anything wrong. It's just important that Ysrael and I have some time alone. Go inside and read and we'll be back in an hour. I promise." I reached out and touched her cheek. "Please, Suna."

"Mina," Ysrael said, tapping on my window.

I turned to him and smiled, grateful to hear his voice, to see his face. And it wasn't until I finally searched his eyes that I realized how afraid I had been all day. That he might have left. That he would have gone without me.

I rolled down the window. "Get in," I said to him and then turned to Suna. I touched her arm. She kept her head down, opened the car door and stepped out into the rain.

I drove us to the lookout. Ysrael sat beside me, his arm draped along the back of my seat, holding on to my headrest. At every red light, I turned to him, checking to make sure he was still there, that he was real. The dampness of his shirt made the goose bumps on his arms rise up. I reached out and touched them.

"You cold?" I asked.

He shook his head. "Nah. I'm fine."

When I finally stopped the car and turned off the engine, I couldn't find any other words except, "I'm sorry."

He stared out the windshield. The clouds enveloped the city, and as night approached, the grayness darkened even further. The soft slanting rain threaded the air.

"I wanted to say something," I said.

"Whatever," he said with a shrug.

"I'm so sorry," I whispered again.

"Did you tell her the truth after I left?" he asked.

I slowly shook my head, no.

Ysrael turned away from me, but not before I saw the look of hurt and disappointment etched on his face.

"I'm leaving tomorrow," he stated without looking at me.

I pulled on his arm. "I'll tell her tonight. I'll get her to ask you back. Ysrael, please."

When Ysrael wouldn't look at me, I leaned forward into the steering wheel and hid my face in my arms. "I'll change," I sobbed. "I'll fix everything. Please don't leave me."

The raw heaves of my breath echoed in the cramped space of the car. I felt Ysrael's hand lightly touching my hair. I turned to him. He wrapped his arms around me and gathered me up, lifting me from my seat and onto his lap.

I buried my face into his neck and let my tears fall across his collarbone, welling up in the hollow. When my cries had finally stopped, Ysrael took one of my hands and held it gently between his palms, as though he had just caught a butterfly. He said, "Come with me."

I thought I could feel the pulse of his heart there in his palms. Felt the wild freedom of that beat traveling up my arm and into my own heart. Imagining a world of my own making. To be free of my lies and Uhmma. To start all over. With

Ysrael. I lifted my eyes and met his gaze. I couldn't take my eyes off him. At the hope that was offered so simply, like a child making a gift of crayon markings on paper. I couldn't face hurting him again.

"Yes," I said.

The rain continued to fall all around us. We were lying down in the backseat, a tangle of limbs and clothes and breaths. Our faces glistening with sweat, shining with wonder. I hovered above him, staring down at the summer brown of his eyes. One of his arms circled my waist. His other hand reached out for my face, his fingers tracing the arch of my cheekbone, brushing back a stray piece of my hair. He lifted his head as though to kiss me, but instead, licked the tip of my nose. I squirmed in his arms, laughing. He smiled. I lowered myself against his bare chest. He traced the ridges of my spine and lifted his head to kiss me. His lips lingering on mine with the faintest touch. Then gently, so gently, he took my bottom lip between his lips and softly sucked. I closed my eyes and smiled at the sensation. He drew back.

"I've wanted to do that from the day I met you," he said.

"Oh, yeah?" I said and bit my lip, hiding it from him.

"Yeah," he said and placed his thumb on the edge of my mouth. In a slow, purposeful arch, he traced and drew out my bottom lip. The intensity with which he stared at me, his eyes luminous and piercing, made me feel shy all of a sudden. I pressed my face into his neck and tasted the salt of his skin. He held me close, never pressing for anything more. He held me in his arms. For a minute. An hour. A lifetime.

I awoke with a start. Darkness filled the car.

"Oh, no, what time is it?" I sat up and grabbed my shirt from the floor of the car. "Suna's waiting."

Ysrael sat up slowly. "You were only asleep for ten minutes," he said.

"Really?" I rubbed my eyes. "It felt like forever."

"That's what happens when you're with me."

"I fall asleep," I joked and leaned in to kiss him.

He faked a hurt look and turned away.

I kissed his cheek and said reluctantly, "I have to get back soon."

"Mina," Ysrael said.

"Hmm," I answered, preoccupied with finding my keys.

"I want you to listen to something," he said and reached into the back pocket of his jeans. He pulled out a cassette. "I finished the song. The one I was working on at the beach. Will you listen to it?"

I nodded and took the tape, turning it over in my hands. Ysrael's name was written along the spine of the tape cover and on the front was my name.

"Why does it feel like you're trying to say good-bye," I tried to joke.

Ysrael shrugged, his face barely visible in the darkness, but I could still see the sad smile on his face. "Just in case," he said and touched my cheek.

I held his hand to my lips and kissed his palm, the tears welling up in my eyes.

"If I don't see you tomorrow, I want you to come find me when you're ready. I'm going to be at that music school.

Maybe you can apply to college somewhere in San Francisco."

I started to shake my head. "You won't even remember me by then."

"Mina," Ysrael said, his eyes closing. "I'm not going to forget you. Why do you always put yourself down? So you're not going to Harvard, it's not the end of the world. You'll find another school. Or do something else. But you can't keep lying to everyone. You have to take responsibility for your life, Mina. You have so many choices. You have to see that."

I turned away from him. "I'm trying."

"I don't want to lose you," he said.

"Then stay," I begged. "Why do you have to go?"

He shook his head slowly. "I can't. I have to do this for me. I want to learn how to really write songs and play music."

I nodded. I wanted that for him as well. Ysrael pulled me close. I sank back against him. We stayed that way without speaking. I pressed my ear to his chest and listened to his heartbeats. The slow start, stop rhythm. Forever beginning. Forever ending. His life. My life. Heartbeat. Heart.

suna

She wanders the aisles of the library, running her fingers along the spines of the books. A wet halo on her shirt where the ends of her hair meets the soft cotton fabric. Her sneakers squeaking in protest with each step. Suna wanders the aisles and wonders why there must be a choice. Why one book over another. Why one daughter over another. Why Mina's love and not hers. Why Ysrael and not Suna.

She stops in the middle of the aisle and slowly pulls out a book. Tips it out with her finger and then lets the weight of the book do the rest. She sees the book fall, notes the way it splays out, the pages fanning the air, before it lands on the floor and closes. Suna pulls another book and another book. She does not hear the loud thud as the book hits the floor, does not hear the librarian's chair scraping back. Suna simply feels the thumps, the hard vibration that travels from the floor into her feet and through her body, soothing her nerves. She pulls book after book and lets them fall. Her concentration on each act, each spine that stands straight and proud. The librarian grabs her wrist just as she reaches up to topple another book.

Suna falls to the floor, her body sagging under the weight of it all. Suna falls to the floor, a book clutched to her chest, and finally cries.

mina

Suna sat on the steps of the library under the overhang. Her arms were wrapped around her legs, her shoulders hunched forward, her body balled up as though she were trying to make herself disappear. Had she been sitting there all that time? I bit my lip in guilt. I should have come back for her sooner.

I started to open my door, but Ysrael touched my shoulder.

"Let me talk to her," he said. "I want to say good-bye."

I nodded.

As he turned to leave, I caught up his hand. "Come back to me afterward. Okay?"

"Don't worry. I'm not going to disappear." He slipped his hand from mine and stepped out of the car.

I watched him run across the parking lot, the rain darkening his hair, his shirt. Suna stood up as she watched him approach. He took the steps two at a time and bulldozed her in a hug. Her face lighted with surprise, her mouth opening, her eyes growing wide.

I muttered, "I hope she has her hearing aid in."

Ysrael took both of her hands in his. He leaned in next to her ear. Suna cast her face to the ground. I could see her taking it all in. Her shoulders slumped forward and a small frown began to crease her forehead. The corner of her lip caught in her teeth. Ysrael pulled back and waited until Suna would meet his eyes. He pushed her bangs off her forehead and kissed the top of her head. He gathered her up in his arms, his embrace lifting her onto her toes. He gently set her back down and then, holding her hand, led her back down the steps to the car. He opened the door for her.

Suna sat down next to me, her clothes soaked, her long black hair clinging to her cheeks.

"He's leaving," she said.

"I know," I said.

She nodded, then looked out the window.

Ysrael came to my side of the car. I stepped out into the rain.

"You didn't have to get out," he said. The rain streamed down his face, beaded on his skin, plastered his clothes against his body.

I gazed up at his face, trying to memorize every detail, every scar. And though he stood right before me, a shiver passed through my body. I reached for him. Stood on my toes, laced my fingers behind his neck and kissed him. His arms circled my waist and I could taste the cool rain on his lips. He finally broke away, leaning his forehead on mine.

"Listen to the song," he said.

"I will."

"I'll wait for you at the bus station, Mina."

I closed my eyes. A wild beating like the first flutter of wings before flight took over my heart. I wanted to be with him. To live my own life. To be happy. Could we really do this? Could we really have a life together? Was this what he really wanted? As though reading my thoughts, Ysrael said softly, "Come be with me."

Ysrael watched us leave. He stood in the rain and waved as I drove out of the parking lot and onto the street. Suna waved and waved even after he had disappeared from our sights.

We stepped inside the apartment to find Uhmma sitting on the couch, watching TV. She stood up as soon as we entered, her fists immediately coming to her waist.

Where have you been? she asked.

The instructor was late, so we didn't get started on time, I said, taking off my wet shoes.

Suna fled to our room.

Uhmma started her lecture: I have been worried. You could have called. I was about to go and look for you. What if something had happened?

I stared at her, my heart racing with the words, the truth. I was with Ysrael. He would never let anything happen to me.

Uhmma shook her head and pushed me. Go and get dry before you catch a cold.

Silently, I left the room, my hand in my pocket, holding on to Ysrael's song. I needed time to gather my courage and finally tell her about Ysrael. And the truth about me.

Suna was still in her wet clothes, standing at the window, her hair dripping water onto the carpet. She turned to me as I entered the room with some towels. I closed the door behind me.

"Are we going to see him again?" she whispered. She wrapped her arms around herself as the shivers crept into her body.

I went to the closet to get some dry clothes for her.

"Uhn-nee, what's going to happen to Ysrael?"

I shrugged.

"Uhn-nee, when Ysrael is in San Francisco and he's looking at the moon, we could be looking at the moon at exactly the same time. We could still be together that way."

I smiled at her thought and brought over her large T-shirt that she liked to wear for pajamas. She changed out of her clothes, letting the wet ones fall to the floor, and she slipped into her T-shirt. I picked up her wet clothes and took my pajamas to the bathroom.

After draping our clothes on the tub, I finally looked at myself in the mirror. I wondered if my skin still tasted of him. I touched my neck. Was his smell still a part of me? Or had the rain washed all of that clean? I closed my eyes and pictured the black dust of his lashes. The ragged edges of his scar. I raised my fingertips to my chin and remembered the pressure of his thumb on the edge of my lips. The thought of Ysrael leaving without me filled me with such sadness, it caught my breath. What was I going to do?

Suna was still standing at the window when I returned from the bathroom. Her long wet hair was soaking her nightshirt. The memory of her sitting under the overhang at the library lifted my hand in guilt. I pulled the towel from my hair and called to Suna.

"Come sit down, Suna," I said and patted her bed. She sat down next to me and I began to towel her hair dry. It had been a while since we had actually spent time together alone like this. The comfort of her presence, the ease of being together. Could I really leave her?

"Uhn-nee."

"Yes, Suna."

"Are you going to miss Ysrael?"

"Yes."

"Do you love him?"

I paused, then answered. "Yes."

"Then why is he leaving?"

I kept toweling her hair dry, keeping her back to me so that she wouldn't see the tears.

"He wants to find his own life. He wants to go to school and make music."

"And he can't do that here?"

I combed my fingers through her hair, gently working out a large tangle. "He doesn't think so. El Cajon isn't much of a city compared to San Francisco. There's a lot more to do and see in a big city like that. Just a lot more opportunity."

Suna remained silent as I finished with her hair. She turned around as I stood up.

"Do you wish you could go with him?" she asked.

I blinked. My heart spoke before I had a chance to think. "Yes."

I waited until Suna was asleep, her breathing slow and steady, before listening to Ysrael's song. I sat up and put the headphones on. A soft guitar melody, the one that I remembered hearing him play at the beach, only now it was more purposeful, more complete. He had just been creating it back then. I drew up my legs and wrapped my arms around them, rested my chin on my knee. Ysrael began to sing to me.

I can see a little bit of your face
In those stars
I can hear a little bit of your voice
In the rustling trees
I can taste a little bit of your lips
On my lips

Am I going mad?
Walking past the car
Keys in my hand
Looking up at strangers
Did you call my name?
Find me some words
Find me a phrase
A book that explains
All this away
'Cause I don't know how . . .

I can hear a little bit of your charm
In my laugh
I can feel a little bit of your touch
In my grasp

I can hold a little bit of your hope
In my dreams

Am I going mad?
Walking past the car
Keys in my hand
Looking up at strangers
Did you call my name?
Find me some words
Find me a phrase
A book that explains
All this away
'Cause I don't know how . . .

I've spent my days
Searching
For a home that surrounds
Eases the soul
All this time
All this wandering
For a place
Four walls, a roof, a porch that creaks with the weight
When
All I needed was
You

I found the words
I found a phrase
It's not a book that explains
The way
The way

I can feel a little bit of your heart
In my heart
I can hold a little bit of your love
In my love

My love.

suna

*S*una jolts awake. Her first thought is that Mina has left. Has gone to be with Ysrael. She rolls over onto her side, her eyes immediately landing on the sleeping huddled form of her sister. Even in the predawn filtered light, Suna knows that familiar shape. The sound of her breathing. All her life, Suna has looked to Mina like a sailor that navigates by the stars. She cannot remember a time when Mina was not there.

Suna adjusts her pillow and then notices the cover of a tape on the floor. She gets out of bed. The black scrawl on the tape cover, the handwriting does not look familiar. It does not belong to Mina and yet her name is written across the front as though it was the name of the album. Suna turns over the empty case in her hands and notices some more writing on the inside cover: 11:00 A.M. Bus #473.

A chill, like a drop of cold water, rolls down the base of her neck. She turns the case over and finds his name along the spine of the cover. Ysrael. Suna sits down on her bed, presses the tape cover to her lips. Her breathing comes in rapid pants. Suna grips the tape and stares at Mina's sleeping face. In a single moment, Suna realizes that she is losing both of them. Ysrael and Mina. Mina and Ysrael. The darkness rushes into her body, invades her thoughts, reaches into her heart until she feels herself growing cold. She will hold on to the one she loves best.

She steps out of the room without a sound. Walks down the hall to her parents' room and opens the door. Suna places the tape in Uhmma's sleeping hand.

mina

*M*orning. I bolted up and reached out for the watch that I had placed on the windowsill before falling asleep last night. Still not too late. I sat on the edge of my bed and thought about what to do. Every part of me wanted to go to Ysrael. I could picture him packing, getting ready to head out to the bus station. I never expected Ysrael's absence to feel so much like physical pain. It hurt to think about him being so far away. And as much as I wanted to believe that we could be together again after I finished school, I knew the chances diminished each day we were apart. I would not lose him.

We could do this. I was going to leave anyway, it would just be a year earlier. I would finish school up there and look into some colleges, maybe even the music school. And when I was finally away from here, from Uhmma, I would tell her the truth. Slowly repay all the money I had stolen. I glanced over at Suna's empty bed and then turned to look out the window. The city was wrapped in a coat of mist, an early-morning drizzle that darkened the buildings.

I got out of bed and quickly began to gather a few things. Some clothes, a few favorite CDs and my player. I reached into the back of a dresser drawer and pulled out the wad of twenties that I had been saving. I shoved it all into my back-pack. I headed out of the room to wake up Suna and explain why I had to leave.

Uhmma stood in the kitchen.

"Hi, Uhmma," I said, trying to keep my voice steady. What was she doing home? I looked around. Suna was awake. She was sitting on the couch, still in her pajamas.

Uhmma stepped quickly out from behind the kitchen counter. She held up the tape cover.

What is this? she asked.

I pretended I had no idea what she was talking about. How had she found the tape cover? Had she come into the room when I had been sleeping? How could I have been so careless to leave that out? I don't know. Just a tape cover.

She narrowed her eyes and stepped closer to me. This, she said. This has your name on it. And that boy's name. That boy who stole from us. I can read. I can see that he gave this to you.

He wanted me to listen to it.

Uhmma opened the cover and asked, Why does it have the time and a bus number? What were you planning?

Nothing, I protested.

Do not lie to me! Uhmma yelled.

I looked down at the floor.

Suna, Uhmma said. Where was your sister last night?

I glanced over at Suna. She was sitting on her hands, quickly biting her lower lip. She had taken out her hearing aid.

Uhmma yelled, *Suna!*

Suna jumped.

Uhmma waved the tape cover at her. *Where did you get this?* she yelled.

Suna kept rocking back and forth, shaking her head.

I closed my eyes. Suna. Suna had given Uhmma the tape. Why? Why had Suna betrayed me? All the hope that I had felt just moments before evaporated. Fatigue overwhelmed my body. I was so tired. So tired of trying to hold everything together. I dropped my backpack.

Suna was crying, her head still shaking back and forth. "Uhn-nee, I'm sorry. Don't go. Please."

Uhmma shook the tape cover in my face. What has been going on, she shouted. You have been seeing that boy. You have been lying to me, Uhmma cried. Her face was pale and white, spit at the corners of her lips. She raised her hand to slap me but then stopped. She paced the room.

Apa walked into the room, one hand on his back, his steps slow and uneven.

Yah, he said, what is all this yelling?

Uhmma ignored him. She waved her hands at me. What are you thinking? Uhmma asked. You were going to throw away your whole future on that boy. That trash. I will not let you. I will not let you throw away your life like I had to throw away mine.

Shut up, I yelled. It's not true. Just stop it! You have no idea what you are talking about. He's honest. And he's good.

Uhmma pushed me. Go to your room.

Apa stepped toward Uhmma. Yuhbow, he said. Calm down. Let us try and talk.

Uhmma turned to him and yelled, Stop. You have nothing to say here. This is my daughter.

Apa turned his head away.

Uhmma turned back to me and said, Go to your room. Go there until I say you can come out. You are not leaving my sight.

No. I stood my ground. I am sick of having to live your life. You never wanted me or Suna.

I never wanted you, Uhmma said, her eyes pinching at the corners. She raised her head and stared at the discolored ceiling of the apartment. She closed her eyes. She spoke in a controlled hiss. You think I wanted this life? I did this all for you. Uhmma wrung her hands, her voice escalating into a yell. My life. My life. Why do you think I married Suna's father? Why? Because I wanted to live this way? You would have had no life if I had not sacrificed. You would have been an orphan.

Uhmma screamed, I threw away everything to keep you. And this is how you treat me. All this work so that you can turn into some common whore.

STOP! Apa said. He stepped forward. That is enough. Do not force your past on her.

Uhmma dropped her face into her hands.

In that moment, I grabbed my backpack and ran for the door. Down the stairs, across the parking lot. I ran from

Uhmma's ghosts. I could hear Uhmma calling after me, Mina. Mina!

I kept running, down the street, across the intersection. I ran until my breath came in hard knots and I had to lean forward. Ysrael. I had to get to Ysrael. I would just leave my past behind. Step into another world. A sense of release. A lightness of being. I straightened up and continued walking.

The rain plastered my clothes to my body, the cold soaking into my skin. The truth making me shiver. What I had sensed so many years ago was true. My father. My history. Suna's history. All lies. So many lies. I started to cry. Why had Suna given Uhmma the tape? Her betrayal cut at the invisible ties that bound me to one life and not the other. To one person and not the other.

And yet. Each step. Each footfall toward my future rang with regret. For Suna. I thought of her crying, begging me not to go. Oh, Suna. I wiped the rain from my face. Why? Were you afraid I would leave you? I stopped, my vision blurred by the tears streaming down my face with the rain. I imagined her in our room, sitting on the bed, her blank face staring out the window. How much had she heard? How much did she already know? Feel? The truth about our lives, our fathers. What would the knowledge do to her?

In the highest reaches of the sky, the sun peeked out for a minute. Sharp rays of light caught up the raindrops and shaped them into jewels. I raised my face to the warmth, to the sprinkles that kissed my cheeks like liquid sun. I could hear Suna's laugh, "Look, Uhn-nee. Sundrops." I bowed my head. I turned around. For Suna.

suna

*S*he walks alone in the rain. The faded pink pajama bottoms and oversized T-shirt clinging to her small frame, heavy with the weight of water. Her breath breaks inside her chest in an upward heave that strangles a cry escaping from her throat. Gulps of air. Her shoulders rising and falling. How much time has passed? She presses the heel of her hand against the tears that blur her vision. Though her chest still throbs, demanding air, she begins to run again. Looks down at her feet and urges them to fly faster, skim across the pavement.

The city, a dusty camouflage of grays punctuated with dots of colors from traffic lights and swirling neon signs, stretches awake in the early-morning drizzle. In the distance there is the slam of metal gates being pushed aside, revealing cluttered storefronts and display windows. The heartbeat of the city thickens with the heat of summer rising as steam from the streets, with the noise of cars speeding across the freeway, with the multitude of voices and languages rising up to greet each other. The day begins, yet all Suna can see is the memory of a face framed by night. A face so familiar, so loved, she can name each imperfection, each mark as though they are her own.

In the distance, a lone figure walks through the rain. Mina returning. For her. Suna runs forward without a glance, without a thought. To the car rounding the curve of the freeway off-ramp. The road slick with oil and rain. She pumps her arms and wills herself into the light.

Suna steps off the curb.

mina

*I*t was only during the unguarded moments, reaching for a hanger in the closet, searching for a spoon in a drawer, when the memory of Suna stepping off the curb invaded my body and forced me to hold my breath until the moment had passed. The what-ifs like a plague compelling me to check and double-check on Suna. Safe.

Still, even as I smiled and waved at her sitting with Apa watching TV, and Uhmma standing off in the distance enveloped in the fog that surrounded her love for us, I imagined what could have happened. The enormity of what would have happened. If I had not gone back.

Suna's eyes had been narrowed in determination as she ran down the street, no sense of sounds, the approaching car rounding the curve of the freeway off-ramp. Her eyes solely focused on the path that led her to me. I had screamed for her to stop as I ran toward her.

Wait for me!

Suna stepped off the curb.

My heart coiled in terror. I ran at the car. Locked my eyes on the driver, willing him to brake. I punched the air. STOP.

The scream of tires. Suna's horror. The realization, the glimpse at another fate skidding past, knocking her down to her knees. I closed my eyes. An awareness of time passing and the muscle of my heart working like a fist. Open close. Heart beat. Mina. Suna.

As I walked with Suna back to the apartment, I glanced behind us, at the street. At the intersection where the ghostly figure of me stood marking a place and time. That moment when I stepped through, and though I may have looked and sounded exactly the same, I knew I could never return to who I used to be. And I grieved for her then. For what she had missed, for the people she had hurt. For the lies she had told herself to make it all worth it.

I set out with Suna, the sun breaking through the clouds, the light resting on our shoulders. For above all else, through all the deceit, there had been this love. Our love. I had to know that Suna would be all right when I finally left. That there was peace in the family, the suffocating past set to rest. It would be one fight after another, but I knew there was no other way. I had to face the truth. I couldn't lie anymore.

There's never a clean cut, running from one life for another. There was always devastation. I just wouldn't have seen it if I had left. Suna was only beginning to discover her voice. I would not see it extinguished before it even had a chance to gain momentum. I reached for her hand. Caught it up in a swing that raised our arms to the sun.

I thought of Ysrael then. I could hear the faint sounds of his music in the rustling trees. His voice lighting on a breeze. And I could feel my own voice rising up inside, deep and light, free yet weighted with an honesty that could only come from taking on the obstacles, the responsibilities of living a life that was true. The street hummed right along to my song.

epilogue

He calls her in the late afternoon, at the one time when he
knows only she will answer. He can picture the front counter
phone ringing loudly next to the cash register. His hands slick
with sweat, a nervous rush of blood to his ears. He calls her to
say that he can't let her go. That he is sorry for having asked
her to choose.

He can't move forward or backward or sideways. Can't do
anything but sing as though she is sitting next to him, her
shoulders turned slightly in a thoughtful gesture of privacy.
The way she did on the beach. That first time they were together. He still goes back to that evening. Places himself on the
beach and sings her a song. It's the only way he knows how to
play now. He calls her to tell her all this, but when he hears her
voice on the other line, hears that familiar catch, that soft
sleepiness in her hello. He can only say quietly, "Hey."

She registers his voice in the jump of her heart before her
memory can even find his name. But when she finally steadies
herself enough to speak, the words that spill forth are not the
words that she has rehearsed a hundred, a thousand, a million
times in her head. The words that part her lips are more real,
more honest and hers alone.

"Wait for me," she asks.

He closes his eyes and sees her as she was that day on
the beach.

Her face lifted to the sun. Her body leaning forward into the music, ready to take flight.

"Always," he answers.

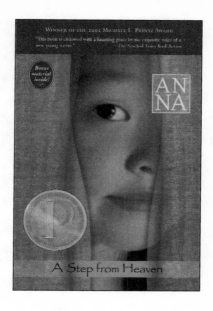

Turn the page to read more about
the first remarkable novel from

AN NA

A Step from Heaven

Sea Bubble

Just to the edge, Young Ju. Only your feet. Stay there.

Cold. Cold water. Oh. My toes are fish. Come here. Fast. Look. What is it, Young Ju?

See my toes. See how they are swimming in the sea? Like fish. Yes, they are little fat piggy fish.

Ahhh! Tickles.

Come on. Up. Keep your legs around me. Are you ready to go swim in the waves?

Hold me. Hold me.

I have you. Look over there, Young Ju. See how the waves dance. See? Hold on tight. We are going over there.

No. Stop. Deep water. Go back.

Shhh, Young Ju. Do not be afraid. You must learn how to be brave. See, I have you.

No. No. Go back.

Young Ju, can you be brave? Look, that is only a small wave. Do not worry. I will hold you tight the whole time. Can you try to be a brave girl for me?

I will try.

Good girl. Ready for the wave? Here it comes. Get ready. Up. And down. There, do you still want to go back?

Again. Do it again. Another one.

That is my courageous girl. Hold on to my neck, Young Ju. Here we go. Up. And down.

I am a sea bubble floating, floating in a dream. Bhop.

All This Weight

Apa is not happy.

Uhmma is not happy.

Halmoni, who is old and has a sleepy blanket face, says that a long time ago Apa was young like me and she could boss him around. But not anymore.

Now, Halmoni can only shake her head when Apa comes home late stinking like the insides of the bottles that get left on the street. Her lips pinch tight, then she hides with Uhmma and me. Because when Apa is too quiet with the squinty eye, it is better to hide until he falls asleep or else there will be breaking everywhere. Halmoni always says, That Apa of yours needs a good spanking. If only your Harabugi had not passed away.

But sometimes when Uhmma is tired of playing sleep, she stops hiding. I pull on her arm. Try to make her get back under the covers. Uhmma shakes away my hand. She slides back the rice paper doors. Her voice deep as night asks, Where were you?

I hide under the covers because the breaking is too loud, too strong. It can come inside my head even though my fingers are in my ears. It sits in my chest, hitting, hitting my heart until my eyes bleed water from the sea. Halmoni rocks me in her lap. Talks to Harabugi's picture. She tells him, Do you see what is happening? How could you leave me with all this weight?

Only God Can

Pray, Halmoni says. Pray to God and everything will be better. Put your hands together tight like a closed book. Good. Then say what I taught you, Young Ju. Remember? Dear Father who art in heaven.

Halmoni, where is heaven?

Heaven is where your Harabugi is. He is with God in a place where there is only goodness and love.

Can I go there?

Someday. If you pray and love God. Do you love God?

Yes, I say, even though at church the picture of his face with the dark round money eyes makes me hide behind the bench. But I want to see heaven and Harabugi, so I try to love him.

Is heaven around here? Can we go there tomorrow? I ask.

No, no. Heaven is in the sky and far away. Now pray while I read the Good Book.

I close my eyes and put my hands together tight. I move my lips the way I see Halmoni do, but without the sounds. God must have very strong ears to hear the words.

Dear Father in heaven.

This is all I remember, so I open my eyes. Halmoni is rocking and reading her Good Book with all the stories about how God came down to be with us. Only when he got here, he said his name was Jesus. I wonder, why did he make up a new name? I wish I could make up a new name, but Halmoni says, Do not be foolish.

I look at Harabugi's picture on the table with the candles all around. He has sleepy eyes like cats in the sun. They are nice eyes.

My Harabugi. Apa has the same eyes. Also the same black hair sticking up straight in the front and flat in the back. I close my eyes and put my hands together tight.

Harabugi, I say with my lips moving but without the sound, if you are in heaven with God maybe you can hear me too. Halmoni says Apa needs a good spanking and there is nobody here to give him one. Could you send God down so he can be Jesus again and give Apa his spanking? Then Apa will be nice all the time. Like when he brought home Mi Shi and Uhmma said, We cannot keep that dog. And Apa said, But she is only a baby doggy. Then he made the baby-doggy face. And Uhmma laughed and pushed Apa on the shoulder. She said, That dog looks just like you. No wonder it followed you home. Then Mi Shi got to stay and be my friend. I like it when Apa is nice and Uhmma makes her squeaky-shoes laugh. Amen.

When I open my eyes Halmoni is looking at me sneaky peek.

That was a long prayer, she says and turns a page. What did you pray about?

That God would come down and give Apa a spanking, I tell her.

Halmoni holds her Good Book tight with both hands. She whispers, He is the only one who can.

Mi Gook

Mi Gook. This is a magic word. It can make Uhmma and Apa stop fighting like some important person is knocking on the door. Dirty brown boxes all tied up, with big black letters in the middle and little pictures all in the corner. They come from Mi Gook. Uhmma says they are from my Gomo. She is older than Apa. His big Uhn-nee. Inside the boxes there are funny toys for me. Like the one that plays tinkle-tinkle music and the scary man with rainbow paint on his face and hair jumping out.

Apa says that in Mi Gook everyone can make lots of money even if they did not go to an important school in the city. Uhmma says all the uhmmas in Mi Gook are pretty like dolls. And they live in big houses. Much bigger than the rich fish factory man's house in the village. Even Ju Mi, my friend who is one year older and likes to boss me around, says she would like to go to Mi Gook.

Then one day Apa gets a letter that makes him hug Uhmma so tight her eyes cry. Now every time Apa says Mi Gook, he smiles so big I think maybe he is a doggy like Mi Shi. When we are eating our dinner, Apa and Uhmma can only say Mi Gook all the time. No more mean eyes over the rice bowl, and my stomach keeps the rice inside like a good stomach is supposed to do. I hope they will talk about Mi Gook forever and ever.

Mi Gook is the best word. Even better than sea or candy. But then when I go to Ju Mi's house to play with my new ball from Gomo, Ju Mi pushes me away.

She says, You are moving to Mi Gook and I feel so sorry for you because you have to leave everything behind.

I bounce my ball and think Ju Mi is talking, talking like she always does. Ju Mi takes the ball away and yells, Did you hear me? You are moving.

What? I yell at her and try to get my ball back.

Stupid. You are moving to Mi Gook.

No, I am not, I say, even though I do not know what moving means.

Stupid baby, she says. You do not even know you are moving away. Your uhmma told my uhmma today. I am happy you are moving so I do not have to play with a baby all the time.

I do not understand why Ju Mi says she is happy when her smile is sticking on her face upside down. I run away to find Uhmma.

Uhmma is outside in the yard squeezing laundry. I pull on her arm and say, Uhmma, Ju Mi says we are moving to Mi Gook.

Sit down, Uhmma says and sits back on her feet, butt close to the ground, knees sticking up to the sky.

I sit back on my legs next to her.

Young Ju, Uhmma says, you know we will be moving to Mi Gook soon.

No, I say. What is moving?

Your Apa and I have been talking about Mi Gook at dinner for days now.

Yes, Uhmma. But you never told me about moving. Does it mean we are going to see Gomo like when we went to see your uhmma and apa?

No. Moving is not like when we went to visit your Eh-Halmoni and Eh-Harabugi. Moving means we will live in Mi Gook forever.

Forever?

Yes.

Where is Mi Gook? Can I still come back to see Ju Mi?

Uhmma pets my hair. No, Young Ju. Mi Gook is far across the sea. We will have to take an airplane that flies in the sky to get there. I do not think you will be able to see Ju Mi for a long time. Uhmma stands up slowly. Aigoo, she says as she always does when her legs hurt from sitting too long.

I keep sitting. I am thinking if I do not see Ju Mi every day then she will find a new friend. Someone who is not a baby. Maybe that new girl with brown pebble teeth. And what about my house? Who will take care of my small house that sits like a hen on her nest? Thinking about leaving Ju Mi and my house by the sea makes my heart hurt. Like someone is poking it with a stick. Ahya.

But then my eyes find the sky. Think about flying up, up, up. Now I know where we are going. I want to run around, wag my tail like Mi Shi. God is in the sky. Mi Gook must be in heaven and I have always wanted to go to heaven. It is just like the Good Book says. All people who love God will go to heaven someday. I love you, God, I whisper. In heaven you have to wear your Sunday dress every day so you can look pretty for God. Ju Mi must be mad because she wants to be me. Ju Mi likes to look pretty all the time and her uhmma lets her dress up only for church.

Uhmma hangs up the wet clothes. She sings soft and tickly as seagull feathers. My eyes are so wide I think maybe they will fall out. Uhmma never sings. Not even in church. She says singing takes too much heart and her heart is too heavy to give to God.

What are you singing, Uhmma?

Ah-me-ri-ka.

What is that?

Mi Gook.

This is a magic word.

F
NA

Na, An
Wait For Me

	DATE DUE		ya
10/7/11			
12/15/11			
2/7/13			
FEB 03 '17			
JAN 06			
SEP 2 REC'D			

WITHI

Book c

m